Short Trips
for Long Trips

Journey from Memoir to Fantasy

Alice Louise

Mind's Eye Media, LLC
Grove City, Ohio

Short Stories for Long Trips:
Journey from Memoir to Fantasy

Copyright © 2014 by Alice Louise

All rights reserved. No part of this publication may be reproduced in any form, stored in a retrieval system, copied in any form or by any means, electronic, mechanical, photocopying, recording, or otherwise transmitted without the prior written permission of the author and the publisher, except where permitted by law.

Front Cover Design: SelfPubBookCovers.com/RLSather.
All rights reserved.
Formatting by Anessa Books

ISBN-10: 0692328769
ISBN-13: 978-0-692-32876-7

PRINTED IN THE UNITED STATES OF AMERICA

Published by Mind's Eye Media, LLC
Grove City, Ohio
mindseyecols@yahoo.com

DEDICATION

I dedicate this book to the Gulf Coast Writers' Group of Bradenton, Florida, whose skillful members helped me to better my writing via their courteous critiques and invaluable suggestions.

CONTENTS

MUCH ADO AT THE WILD TURKEY CAFÉ 5
UNCLE WALT AND THE EASTER BUNNY 9
THE YELLOW PARASOL 12
MY FAMILY TREE 17
CRYSTAL 25
UNEXPECTED DETOUR 28
SWEET STRANGER 35
SIDESHOW 38
DO NOT DISTURB 49
CARRIE 52
RUN AWAY 55
THE MECHANICAL MAN 57
KEEP THE CHANGE 82
THE RETURN 90
MAUSOLEUM 94
THE FINGER OF GOD 101
HUSH...104
WINTER SOLSTICE 118
UNFORGIVEN 120
A SOFT PLACE TO FALL 124
IF YOU CAN'T STAND THE HEAT 128
SISTERS...133
FOR LOVE 138
THE RIALTO 142
A SWALLOW'S PLACE 146

MUCH ADO AT THE WILD TURKEY CAFÉ

"Entrapment" is an ugly word at the Wild Turkey Café. Now don't get me wrong; that's not the only ugly word at the Wild Turkey. There's also, "You've had enough," sometimes voiced by the ever-present Julio, the bartender. Or, "Drink up. The bar is closing."

All of these words cause a general grumbling among the regular patrons. Of late, however, *entrapment* ranks up there with "shut off his/her drinks!"

First, I should tell you that the Wild Turkey Café is no different from most neighborhood bars. It's of the kind that has shutters over the windows, a sign on the door warning that you must be twenty-one to enter, and neon beer bottles glowing amber over the doorway. The entrance is dark and odoriferous, the fragrance of old beer and stale cigarette smoke is pervasive. However, to any member of the regular patrons group, this is an aroma that says home.

It's sort of a club, and a tough club to join, that is, if you want permanent membership. The pecking order is strictly followed. Bob (never tell them your name) Casey has been sitting on the third stool from the door for fifteen years—off and on.

At age sixty-five, you might call him the C.E.O. of the Wild Turkey.

If you need an answer to a prickly problem, Bob can give you the answer. Of course, sometimes, he deigns not to answer on the grounds that, as he says, "You really are a dumb S.O.B.!"

Jerry Gibbs, a Lyle Lovett look-alike, is fifth stool from the front. Quiet and much respected in the group, because his brother is a municipal court judge who gives him cigars "for the boys." Gibbs shares them generously each Saturday.

Gino is a tile setter and always looks like he just took a bath in the local quarry—dust covered! He sits near the rear of the bar usually smiling, shaking his head slowly up and down in agreement with Pete Fabio, whose loud mouth gives him the obvious status of Sergeant at arms...or perhaps I should say Sergeant at *arm*. Pete lost one arm as a kid trying to outrun a train. He polices the front entrance, and when strangers show up in the darkness, Pete's voice can be heard shouting,

"Who the hell are they?" Thus, the closed club effect.

Now, getting back to this *entrapment* thing.

Every Thursday is ladies day, and DeeAnn, Sissy, and June, show up early, about 11:30 a.m. These ladies represent the auxiliary members of the Wild Turkey Café. They are welcomed with courtly grace by Bob, a sheepish grin from Jerry Gibbs, an extra nod from Gino, and a smack on the posterior by Pete. They accept the plaudits as their due.

So, one Thursday, things were moving along at the usual pace (slowly), when DeeAnn started to get a little kittenish. She began to kid Pete who, never at a loss for words, dared her to "moon" the 1:35 p.m. freight train, whose rails passed about twenty feet from the back door of the café. Pete bet her three beers that she'd never have the guts.

DeeAnn ordered a boiler-maker and headed for the back door. It was exactly 1:34 when the train whistle blew on down the tracks. As the engineer neared the café, he saw a woman carefully pick her wobbly way toward the tracks. She stopped about eight feet from the rails, dropped her jeans...leaned over and dusted off her boots.

The sight threw the engineer into a spasm of laughter and his fireman nearly choked with glee!

When it was over, DeeAnn wobbled back to the Wild Turkey declaring, "I'm the winner. Pay up!" The group around the bar all tapped their bottles on the bar and declared her the "best mooner in town!"

Thereafter, DeeAnn accepted bets on her, shall we say, audacity, every Thursday afternoon, spurred on by the members present. She collected an unmetered amount of the suds free.

Sissy and June gave her their unselfish support, sharing in her winnings.

Just when the game was becoming barely funny to the club members, DeeAnn gave one last performance before Thanksgiving.

This time, when the freight train passed, two plain-clothes detectives jumped off one of the passing cars and arrested her, handcuffs and all. (Of course, they had her pull up her drawers first.)

DeeAnn was charged with a misdemeanor; "exposing her private parts," and her bail was set at three hundred dollars.

The Wild Turkey patrons were up in arms about the arrest. They pulled together and took up a collection to get poor DeeAnn out of the slammer.

"It ain't fair," Pete bellowed.

"Right!" Gino shook his head.

"I'll speak to my brother." Jerry offered.

Bob ordered a double Seagrams, washed it down with a beer, and declared, "It's entrapment!" Then he explained that the only way they could arrest DeeAnn was if the police saw the act with their own eyes. So, evidently the railroaders had ratted on her.

Bob calmly accepted the job of taking the bail money down to the station and picking up their heroine. He drove her back to the café where she accepted their welcome, while carefully explaining that, "Them railroaders had no right to set me up. They liked it. They tooted the whistle ten times last week!"

Pete smacked her on the tush, as Bob sat very straight and declared, "It's entrapment." Gino shook his head to agree, while Jerry passed out cigars two days early.

Epilogue

The next Thursday, DeeAnn's friend Sissy decided to get revenge on the railroaders. While June held her mammoth-sized, red purse, Sissy, teetering on four inch red heels, stiff-legged it to the tracks behind the Wild Turkey. At 1:33 P.M., the freight passed. Sissy dropped her drawers and screamed, "Arrest me!"

Unfortunately, the police weren't there to see, but the entire gang in the saloon was watching from the back door!

UNCLE WALT AND THE EASTER BUNNY

THE WHOLE FAMILY on my mother's side thought that Uncle Walt was "different." Now, I'd heard other adjectives used to describe him, but the most polite was "different."

When my dad got wound up on a few beers, he was known to express himself on the subject of Uncle Walt in less tactful terms, like "queer duck" or "weird." Nevertheless, we all tried to be as respectful to Uncle Walt as we could be.

Mom said that he married Aunt Genevieve in one of those kinda wild, flower-child ceremonies in the early 1970's. You might know the kind, where some long-haired hippie sat on a pillow playing a sitar and the bride and groom, in bare feet, swore personal homemade vows about the eternal light of their love, while they clutched one symbolic candle between them. Mom said it kinda embarrassed Grandma when they kissed at the end of the ceremony. I guess the kiss was a lulu that lasted about a full minute.

The newlyweds did settle down to domestic life pretty good though, and Uncle Walt managed to father three girls and one son. No way matching the record of Mom and Dad who had eight of us. Me, and my twin brother, being the oldest at fifteen.

There was no hint of trouble in the family until everyone started to notice that every Eastertime, Walt became overly exuberant, decorating their house and trees with colored eggs and hanging purple lights on the evergreens. He painted every other slat on the porch railing yellow and purple. He also took to disappearing for hours on end. Genevieve couldn't find him. Rumors flew. The neighbors hinted that something was, indeed, strange about Uncle Walt's Easter madness each year.

Aunt Genevieve and Mom quietly whispered that maybe he was having an affair! I eavesdropped frequently.

Then, too, there were traces of facial make-up on his Irish face when he returned home. Dad wondered, out loud, (after a few beers), if Walt might be gay or a cross dresser!

Mom promised Dad that she'd never speak to him again if he ever repeated that to anyone.

Aunt Margaret, Mom's sister, came to visit two Easters ago and forced the issue to a head. A heady issue it turned out to be!

It seems that Uncle Walt is, indeed, a cross dresser!

Oh, not quite what you imagine. He has an Easter bunny fetish.

Yep! That's right. An Easter bunny fetish! He finally owned up to it. "Just can't help it," he told Aunt Margaret.

Seems every Easter time he dresses up like the bunny, and sits in the local mall passing out jellybeans to the little kids. Says it gives him a high like he never felt before. He says when he's the Easter bunny he has no worries at all.

Ever since the revelation, the family tries to ignore Uncle Walt's strange, annual behavior. Everyone pretends not to notice. Every Saturday before Easter, Mom lines up all the little ones and heads for the mall. She marches all six of them past the bunny standing there and he shovels out jellybeans. Mom never was one to pass up a good thing.

Since my twin brother and I are too old for that kind of stuff, we stand back and watch, pretending we don't know who he is. Lately though, I'm beginning to wonder if the strange fetish could be in the family genes, 'cause I notice my nose twitching and my feet hopping along much faster as Easter approaches each year!

THE YELLOW PARASOL

MARIETTE ARMBREWSTER started disappearing from her room shortly after she was admitted to Fairhaven Retirement Home. But, I'm a little ahead of my story!

I remember when they brought her to my office to register her.

"My, what a lovely, sunny office you have here." Her blue eyes were smart and brilliant. She was eighty-eight years old. The most beautiful old lady I had ever seen.

"Welcome to Fairhaven!" I held my hand out to her as she was seated opposite me. "We've been looking forward to meeting you. Your son has told us so much about you."

"Not too bad, I hope." Smiling, she nodded to her son Jacob, who was standing nearby to move her walker out of the way.

"I'm Hattie Weiss, and just as soon as we get your lease signed, we'll take you to your lovely, little apartment. You have seen it, haven't you?"

"Oh yes!" She smiled her warm arresting smile, but there was sadness in her eyes.

"Now, you will be able to have your own furniture, as you know. I understand that your son and daughter-in-law are getting you settled in. There are so many little nuisance things to do, setting up your pictures, hanging your clothes... I'm sure you've noticed the closets are very ample."

Mariette listened attentively. A faint fragrance of flowers seemed to fill the room, perhaps her cologne.

"Dinner is at 5 p.m. each day, including Sundays. You may certainly have guests for dinner or lunch as long as we are informed ahead of time, so that we can prepare for them. Breakfast and lunch are served until 1 p.m. If you wish to pass up any meals you may, but we do ask you to tell the floor administrator to that effect."

Tilting her lovely head of angelic white hair toward me she said, "I don't eat much anymore. No appetite."

"Well, we'll just see what we can do to help that! Our cook makes wonderful pastries."

Our talk over, the papers signed, I led Mariette and Jacob toward 'A' wing where her two small rooms were located. Jacob's wife, Dolly, was starting to hang a picture on the wall when we got there. Everything looked quite nice. No ogres here, I thought.

There was something special about Mariette that drew people to her. She sparkled like sunlight on a lily pond. Soft, warm, and appealing. I, too, fell under her spell. I'd been admissions director at Fairhaven for ten years and couldn't remember when I had been so drawn to a resident.

One painting, in particular, she admired so much that she insisted it must be hung on the wall opposite her bed. "I want to wake up in the morning seeing it and go to bed at night looking at it. It's so comforting."

The oil painting was not large. Perhaps 12"x16" in size. A picture of a rural flower garden, riotous with color, a dirt lane led the eye to a lovely English-type cottage, circa late 1800's. Standing by the door of the cottage, a young man held a bouquet of the flowers as if he were waiting for someone to come from the cottage door. He wore a broad-brimmed, yellow straw hat. His nondescript clothes hinted that he was a farmer. A lovely, bucolic scene reminding one of the French impressionists. I did not recognize the artist's name.

It was about a month into her residency when we first noticed Mariette's ability to move around much faster than we expected. One minute she would be in her rooms, it seemed like only minutes later she would show up on the terrace, or in the library, or even the gift shop! All the while, the staff searched for her. She was a gamin!

"Now, now!" she'd say. "You mustn't get so worried about me. I can take care of myself."

Before Christmas, she called me to her rooms to request a favor. Could I buy a pair of large-sized men's overalls...light blue. "Could you have them gift wrapped? There's a friend of mine, who needs them... Could this be just between us?"

"Mariette, what are you brewing?" I laughed. The whole incident seemed innocent and trivial. I got her the overalls and forgot about it.

On Christmas Eve, she failed to show up for our special dinner and party. We all knew she would be going to Jacob's on Christmas Day. Where could she be? We searched everywhere on the premises to no avail, then about 9 P.M., one of the aides found her back in her bed, sound asleep.

The only thing we could get out of her was, "Oh, I just went for a short walk."

"In your nightgown?" I questioned.

Her eyes twinkled up at me. "...I don't remember."

I was beginning to think she was approaching advanced senility!

No further incidents were noticed until Easter-time, when she once again sent for me. We talked at length during this visit, and I remember her telling me how much she missed her home and the quality of life she'd had when Jacob was a boy.

The Yellow Parasol

"You know, times were hard for us then. I can remember taking Jacob on a sightseeing tour of the city. We went up to the top of a skyscraper and he was so excited. As I held his small hand I wished I could fly away with him, you know. I just wished so hard that I could simply take him and disappear from all our troubles. No more worries, just Jacob and me floating away. No more worries..... Isn't that silly?"

Touching her frail shoulder, I assured her that I had, once or twice, wished the same wish.

"I want you to do a small favor for me. Would you try and find me a yellow parasol. I should say, umbrella? Just keep it between us again. A gift for Dolly."

She knew I was a soft touch. So it was that I became her co-conspirator. Of course, I found the yellow parasol for her.

The next thing she talked me into was sending for a straw bonnet she'd seen in a country magazine. I never asked why she wanted it.

Things at Fairhaven were going well. No complaints about the food or the help for over two weeks. Then, Mariette turned up missing again, only this time it was very different. She'd left me a note. All it said was, "Wishing can really make it so! Please keep my sweet painting for yourself. With Love, Mariette!"

Nonplussed and sick at heart, I helped search for days hoping to find her... fearing we'd find her... wishing she'd return on her own again. After two months, the police quit looking. We gave up.

Jacob honored her note and gave me the lovely painting, which I had difficulty looking at for a long time. I hung it on the wall opposite my desk in my office.

Early in January the next year, we got an unusual thaw. It was like spring, and as I sat in my office, looking out at the sunshine, my eyes wandered back to the painting. I looked at it, staring, trying to understand why it looked so different to me. The flowers were more brilliant than jewels. The dirt lane, more real than before, led my eyes once again to the cottage lit by sunlight. The farmer stood there, as before, the bouquet he held was as fresh looking as his new-looking blue overalls. Stepping through the doorway, a girl with platinum curls peeking out from under an old fashioned, straw bonnet was opening a yellow parasol. The bonnet hid her face.

I wondered if I was losing my mind. I'd never noticed the girl before, but the yellow parasol I knew at once. How could that be? Suddenly, I remembered Mariette's words. "Wishing hard enough can make it so."

MY FAMILY TREE

THE HOUSE I was raised in didn't look like it had a jinx on it. It had a beautiful, tall magnolia tree that brought forth gorgeous, blood-red blooms; most unusual. People used to drive by our home just to see the tree when it bloomed.

The tin-roofed ranch-style house was built in 1858 and bore the eclectic architectural tastes of each generation of Potters who'd inherited it and then enlarged it.

It was the kind of dwelling that seems to stay attached to one family like a maiden aunt of old. Hard to keep, impossible to get rid of. A place in a storm, and it saw lots of those.

It had its secrets, too, and maybe it had been jinxed.

The story is told that Isobel O'Hara had married my great grandfather, Josiah Potter, on a dare. Isobel was headstrong and beautiful, the youngest of two sisters.

It was customary, in those days, for the eldest daughter in the family to marry first. The Potters and the O'Hara's were long-time close friends, so it seemed natural that the Potters' son, Josiah, would marry the staid, older sister, Dora O'Hara. The friendship between Dora and Josiah was a long lasting one. Love was never mentioned.

The engagement secured and the wedding imminent, the families pooled their resources and energy to build a small house for the newlyweds on a parcel of land that was a gift from the Potters.

Isobel watched the proceedings with smoldering green eyes, coveting every board and nail that was part of the new house. Her jealousy was kept well hidden from other members of the family. But the fear that she would end up as a maiden lady was a constant worry to her.

A long planned visit from their cousin, Jessie, only helped to reinforce her fears of old-maidenhood.

The two girls were of an age. They even looked alike as cousins often do. Their red hair and milky skin gave them an angelic look. Isobel and Jessie were closer than sisters.

"How'd you let that handsome, tall man get away from you?" Jessie taunted Isobel.

"Do you really think he's that good lookin'?"

They giggled about it a lot.

Then, as the lazy afternoons brought the cousins more time to speculate about the injustices of life, Jessie tossed off the dare to Isobel.

"Bet you couldn't have gotten him anyway... even if you had been born first."

Isobel, already smarting as a second-placer said, "I'll bet you I still can!"

"Don't be silly, Isobel. It's too late...," then, "all right, I dare you to try."

That balmy evening had a full moon that drenched the O'Hara farm like a beacon. The Gulf, although nearly a quarter of a mile away, could be heard dashing itself roughly toward the sandy shoreline.

Josiah, after a walk with Dora, bid her goodnight at the O'Hara's front door with a perfunctory kiss.

Walking carefully in the moonlit lane, Josiah hadn't gone more than a hundred yards when he heard weeping. Cautiously, he rounded a bend in the narrow dirt road fearing a wildcat or worse. Instead, he saw something move under a high pine tree. A

My Family Tree

closer look told him the weeping was, indeed, not a wildcat but his sister-in-law to be, Isobel O'Hara, standing against the tree.

Rushing to her rescue, "My dear, are you all right. What can I do?" Josiah was very conciliatory.

Lovely Isobel, her tearless face covered by both of her tiny hands, her lovely slim body seeming to be wracked with sobs and lingering sighs, held her arms out to Josiah for his comforting and didn't let go until almost dawn.

The engagement of Dora O'Hara and Josiah Potter ended the same week the house was finished, three months after Isobel arranged to have herself rescued from her imaginary misery.

A month after the broken engagement, Isobel and Josiah were married by the circuit preacher, in a quick and quiet ceremony. Cousin Jessie held the bridal bouquet as the couple exchanged rings.

If sister Dora held spite over the broken engagement and the betrayal by her own sister, she never showed it. For a wedding gift, she presented the bride and groom with a fine magnolia sapling with blooms of a rare color—almost as red as blood. It was planted about twenty feet from the front porch of what was once to have been Dora's home.

Dora never married.

Isobel hated the tree. It stood as a constant reminder of her own duplicity.

Five months after the wedding, Noble Potter was born to Isobel and Josiah. It was, of course, a premature birth.

He was always sickly, making Isobel dote on him more than usual. She controlled his food and rest like a drill sergeant. Poor Noble suffered from extremes of acidity and croup.

As the only child of Isobel Potter, young Noble had very little life of his own. By the time he had grown to a marriageable age, Isobel had already picked the girl for him.

"Noble, darlin', you're just going to love Priscilla Turley. She's such a jewel, and so pretty." His mother's green eyes sparkled. "She's Judge Turley's daughter. Such a nice family."

The Turleys were duly invited for a Sunday dinner.

They accepted. It was the first of many dinners shared by the Potters and the Turleys. Priscilla and Noble seemed quietly compatible, if not infatuated.

The pact was made and the engagement was to be announced within two weeks. A few days later, Noble disappeared from the ranch and wasn't heard from for five days. He'd done this several times during the last few months, making Isobel nearly crazy. He never explained.

The morning of the fifth day of her son's disappearance, Isobel was sitting on the satin covered window seat in the airless parlor, gazing out at the blood-blossoms of the magnolia tree. The morning fog was lifting as she saw Noble riding slowly up the lane to the house on his favorite horse.

"Noble! Noble! My darlin' boy, where have you been?" She ran out the front door, her red-sausage curls bobbing.

Smiling broadly, Noble Potter waved at his mother as he dismounted beneath the magnolia tree. Behind him, on a smaller horse, a tiny young Indian woman waited for Noble to help her dismount. She was exquisitely beautiful. Her black hair shining in the first rays of the morning sun. She was also very pregnant.

"Mother, I want you to meet my wife."

His mother found her tongue with difficulty. "Surely you are trying to joke with me?" Her eyes appraised the tiny woman.

"No, ma'am, this is no joke. Her name is Little Flower, but I call her 'Maggie' for Magnolia."

Isobel seriously considered fainting at that point, but decided it wouldn't do much good. It was all too obvious that Noble had known this squaw for quite some time...way past fainting time.

"Surely you don't intend for her to come here and live with us?"

"Well, I figured we'd either live here or I'd have to go back to the Everglades and learn how to hunt and fish."

"But, Noble, darlin', you could never live like that... not without your Mama lookin' out for your diet and all."

She looked into her son's eyes and knew it was no use to fight this abomination. She saw that Noble, having failed to inherit her robust health, had nevertheless inherited her stubborn determination.

Little Flower entered Potter House with her husband's arms around her and her mother-in-law's passive resistance surrounding her like threatening dark clouds. For many years, for Isobel, the strained truce would be one of the mind, but not of the heart, lifting only slightly after the arrival of Maggie's first born.

It was 1900 when my own mother, Sara, was born to Maggie. My mama was a true throwback, with dusty, olive skin and hair the black of a summer storm cloud. She was the third and last of Maggie's brood, all girls. They called her Sara Isobel in honor of two grandmothers. Everyone called her Sade.

The First World War was coming to an end when Sade met Buford Jones at a church picnic. He had lately returned from military service in Europe and took to Sade right away, putting stars in her eyes and a yearning in her heart.

That was 1918. That year the Magnolia tree seemed to grow taller and its mystical red blooms grew more profusely than ever before. The soft, balmy Gulf Coast breezes scattered the petals of the tree's blood-red blooms everywhere around the house.

Mama always hated the tree, saying that it was, "a dirty thing. It makes a gooey mess on the walk."

Pushing a broom over the dropped blooms, she complained, "Just look at the stain on the rugs from people's shoes."

Sometimes, mothers and daughters are lucky enough to have the kind of close relationship Mama and I had. The kind of confidential trust in each other, knowing whatever we confided in one another would be just between us.

One day, when she was complaining bitterly about the magnolia tree, I asked her right out, why she hated the beautiful old tree so much.

"That tree cost me the love of my life!" She stuck her chin out in that stubborn, familiar way she had when she was upset. But a new defiance shown from behind her dark eyes.

I sat transfixed. Always, I'd thought my daddy was the only man who'd ever been in Mama's life.

This new Sade sat at her dressing table looking at me through the reflection in the mirror. Her countenance was dark and ominous.

Sitting myself down on the end of her bed, I just couldn't find anything to say.

"His name was Buford Jones and we were engaged to be married. One afternoon that spring it rained something awful and the petals from the magnolia tree fell to the ground in bunches like this year. The front sidewalk was gooey with them."

She stopped talking for a minute as she dug through the vanity drawer and pulled out a lacy handkerchief. A few tears streamed down her dusky, sun-kissed cheeks. She dabbed them away with the hanky.

"When Buford came by one evening to call, he slipped and fell on the damned things and broke his leg. We took him to the hospital in town where he would have good care. Daddy paid for it all. He was in the hospital three days."

"Did you visit him every day, Mama?"

"Every day."

"Then what?"

"Molly Sykes, a recently returned nurse from the front in Europe, was Buford's nurse. She took real good care of him." Mama was hardly able to continue her story, she was crying so hard.

It seemed that about the third day of Buford's stay at the hospital, he got his crutches and the two veterans disappeared together. Mama said they didn't even leave her a note.

"That damn magnolia tree is a curse!" she wept.

Yesterday, I awakened to a beautiful May morning.

I could smell sweet gardenias in the air and a mockingbird was singing its soul out.

In three days, on May 9, 1949, I would marry my sweetheart, Thomas, the love of my life. What more could I ask for?

Suddenly a horrible grinding sound came rushing through my open window, scaring me fully awake.

I jumped out of bed and hung over the window sill, my bleary eyes searching for the noise maker. There, in front of the house, Mama stood like an aproned general, her black Indian hair in a fat braid down her back, yelling over the uproar to Tom Meets.

Tom, local tree surgeon, held onto his busy chainsaw.

"Cut it clear to the ground!" Mama ordered.

"Are you sure, Sade?... It's a mighty purty tree."

"Yes, I'm sure...clear to the ground and haul it all away."

I couldn't believe that Mama was having the old magnolia destroyed. Why? I asked myself. Then my eyes wandered toward the closet door in my room. The door stood open. Over the top of the door, a dress hanger clung, wearing my wonderful wedding gown. MY Tom's picture smiled at me from the frame on my nightstand. I had to decide whether to laugh or cry.

Mama was taking no chances on my future!

CRYSTAL

WE SIT SCRUNCHED UP together in the cell. It stinks of perspiration, booze and cloying cheap perfume. The kind of perfume my kid brother used to give to Ma for Christmas. But this ain't Christmas, and I ain't the Madonna.

The cell, meant to hold four women, holds seven tonight. Every once in a while, "Beasty," the woman guard, walks by watching us. Every time she does, Queenie jumps up to the bars begging for a cigarette, while "Ticonderoga" (ex-school teacher, ex-wife, and now chief bag lady of the area) spits tobacco juice at Beasty's feet. Every time they try to take the chewing tobacco away from Ticonderoga, they can never find it. God knows where she hides it.

Her AKA name came from the papermill town she's from in north New York State. I think the farty smell of the paper mill rubbed off on Ty.

I sit on the edge of a dirty bunk mattress wondering to myself how I got into this mess. These women are a reflection of where I've been and where I'm headed.

"Baby" sittin' over there, blubbering, was me, five years ago. This is her first arrest for prostitution and she's scared to death. Her ass-high mini skirt is crumpled. Her red spike-heeled shoes are new. Her red hair reminds me of Orphan Annie.

Tomorrow, tomorrow, there ain't no tomorrow, it's always a life away. Baby, don't know nothin' about that stuff yet.

How many times have I been put in this rat hole? Fifteen? Twenty? Thirty? I've lost count.

Beasty comes up to the cell door. "Okay, Queenie, lover-boy brought the cash to bail you out."

Queenie sleepwalks through the cell door. She leers at the guard, "I knew I'd never spend the whole night in lock-up." Like it was some accomplishment!

That'll be me in a few years. No great expectations left.

Queenie will be lucky if lover-boy don't beat the hell out of her for getting busted.

Me? I'm a free spirit. Always was. I work my own corners and ain't obligated to no one. The only trouble with that is when I get busted, I have to go through the whole court mess and pay my own fine. But, no one knocks me around.

Why don't I get out?

Out to what? Who's interested in a twenty-five-year-old hooker for anything but hookin'...'specially these days.

Ma used to try and get me out but she's dead now. My kid brother died in 'Nam. There ain't no one else.

I've forgot how to cry. Prayin' doesn't seem to work for someone like me.

I put the sweater I had tied around my shoulders, down around my cold legs and lean back against the dirty cement wall. Lipstick graffiti is smeared, unreadable. It decorates the walls.

I must have finally dozed off when Beasty comes to the cell door again. She runs those red-rimmed eyes over us like a ferret. "Crystal! Crystal! A lawyer is here to bail you out. Move it!"

Pinching my eyes shut, I don't move.

Beasty screams again, "C'mon Crystal, I said you been rescued!"

Turning over on my side I look over at the beast-woman and start to get up. Whizzzz, just like that, she ain't there when I look again. Hell! She wasn't there in the first place. Imagine me dreamin' anything good in this friggin' place.

Ticonderoga picks this very minute to puke all over the floor. It's going to be a long night.

UNEXPECTED DETOUR

HIGHWAY 75, south from Cleveland, Ohio, drifted past the car windows in a fast-forward of boring frames. Billboards announcing eateries, motels, and housing developments unraveled their way down the freeway.

The engine of my red Camaro purred on and on, dependable like William, my soon-to-be husband.

I thought of his darkly handsome face, with the questioning look, when I told him about my plans to visit my mother for two weeks in Florida. "Why go to Florida now?" he asked. "The wedding's only two months away and she'll be here in Cleveland, then."

I told him that I needed to clear my head a little before the wedding. I left him sitting in the living room of my small apartment as I escaped into the kitchenette. Tumbling ice cubes into glasses, I asked myself what was wrong with me. This career nurse should be proud to be engaged to marry William Cash. He was a young and successful attorney.

I took the glasses of soda in to William knowing that the evening would end, as they have so often lately, with an argument between us. Arguments that escalated to hasty, early good nights, as he departed with hurt feelings over something I said or planned that did not agree with his ideas about our wedding!

Here I am, Caroline Fisher, twenty-seven years old, considered to be mature, reasonable and "in love," but am I? There are no skyrockets, bells, or whistles in this relationship but, then, I wasn't sure there should be. I'd never been "in love" before. My respect, admiration, and friendship for William knew no bounds. Shouldn't that be enough?

The grey of evening made me aware that it was time to look for a motel. The freeway exit number for the Holiday Inn was emblazoned on a billboard.

Darkness pulled its shade fast here, as my car hummed around the oval exit ramp toward the motel. It was quite dark. The exit ended at a two-lane highway intersection. A deserted area with confusing signs pointing in all directions. Disappointed that the motel was still five miles to the right, I turned the car west. Behind me, a set of lights approached at a fast rate of speed. The lights were on high and blinded me from my rear view mirror; I turned it to night reflections. Another set of lights was approaching off the exit ramp from which I had just turned. Oh, God! I prayed, they're not going to make it! The two cars were on a collision course!

Watching for the inevitable crash of the two cars in my rearview mirror took on a made-for-replay, slow-motion life of its own. The impact exploded in my ears as one of the autos was hurled into the air rolling toward me. Reacting in the worst possible way, I slammed on my brakes toppling my Camaro over a low guardrail. My car rolled side over side down into a dark ravine. After that, there was only terror. Stillness. Then all went black for me.

I don't know how long I was unconscious. My best guess would be about two hours; the moon was directly overhead. My head pained me... like a bass drum being pounded by a baseball bat; I couldn't move my right leg. It, too, pained me beyond anything I'd ever endured before. I held my head, the darkness was palpable. I wondered if I was dead! Then above me the cacophonic sounds of sirens and the babble of people reached my ears. I was alive but no one came to help me. Didn't they know I was there?

Slowly, the sounds faded away. I lay there, pinned in the car, too weak to cry out.

Couldn't seem to open my eyes because of the head pain. Then, I felt, rather than saw, a brilliant light shining into my closed eyes. Its brilliance was merciless. Something touched my face, brushing against my cheeks and neck. Trying again to open my eyes, I could barely discern someone moving around me. Someone has come to help me! That was my last lucid thought before passing out.

The sensation of being lifted and carried penetrated my foggy mind, that and the soft whirring sounds of an engine.

Wherever they took me there were few sounds, no odors, and as I struggled to open my eyes into narrow slits, I could see no trauma equipment! I struggled with the thought as I strained to look around the room. It certainly looked like a very modern hospital room. Everything shined reflectively, even the walls. I could touch the edge of the gurney I was lying on. Carefully, I turned my head toward the closest wall. My own face peered back at me! My short dark hair matted to my skull, both of my eyes were bruised and swollen nearly shut, which could account for the effort I had to muster to see anything. Somewhere in my crazy, mixed-up thoughts, I wondered if my brown eyes had turned blue. A phenomenon I'd heard about once at the hospital!

I tried to move to get a better look at myself, but found that I was restrained on the gurney. Another jolting sequence of pains in my head blinded me, and once more, the terrible darkness came back.

High-pitched sounds pierced my eardrums. I forced my slit-eyes open as a cool hand touched my brow. Standing beside me was a tall, blonde, young man, his green eyes looking intently into mine with great compassion. He looked to be about my age and was dressed in metallic-like coveralls.

"Please don't be alarmed. We're here to help you." He stood straight like a military man.

I tried to speak, I couldn't. Oh, God! I thought, my leg hurts! The blonde giant held a short silver-colored scepter in his hand. He reached out and carefully passed the little scepter up and down my leg. Almost immediately the pain subsided!

He looked at me, silently; a low moan escaped my lips as I tried again to speak. If only he could stop the pain in my head. The thought had hardly formed when "guardian angel" leaned over me and touched my forehead with a cool hand then the "magic wand."

Blessed rest came to me. I slept painlessly, for what seemed like hours.

Grey figures awakened me, moving around me, ministering to me silently. Another group of shadowy figures stood by observing me... watching everything; inspecting me and my reactions! Frightened, I willed my mouth to open to speak.

"Go away! Go away!" I demanded, in a voice weak and hoarse.

The "healer" appeared at my side touching my hand softly. His eyes riveted on me, I thought, who are you... why am I here?

"My name is Palu." He answered my unspoken questions. "You are here until they come for you."

Until they come for me? I looked up into Palu's eyes and knew that he would never allow harm to come to me. How I sensed that I'll never know, but I knew this man and trusted him completely!

Guilt plagued me even in my misery. This should be a time when I wanted and needed William! Good, kind, dependable William, who never allowed me to call him "Bill." I should be thinking of him as my protector, not this giant-of-a-man who hypnotized me with his gentleness and caring,

Suddenly I could hear the quiet whirring sound I'd listened to when I was moved from the wreck to this place. It seemed like eons ago; I had no way to tell how long I'd been cared for in the shimmering room. Things were becoming blurry to me again. My eyes wouldn't focus, my body felt leaden.

Palu stood beside me once more, lifting my limp hand, caressing it. "We're taking you back now, Caroline. It's time."

If he'd slapped me across the face, the blow wouldn't have been more shattering to me. I realized that this man was everything I had ever looked for in a doctor, but even more in a man. I cried out at him, straining to sit up... to hold on to him! Some inner voice screamed out... I needed him! He held my hands firmly but gently until I became quiet again. Rolling my head toward him, I pleaded with my eyes.

"I can't come with you to your world and you don't belong in mine." Quietly, he whispered, "You will forget this."

Looking at him through my swollen eyelids, I could not quite comprehend what he was saying to me. I clutched at him, tearing a small piece of cloth from the pocket of his coveralls.

His arms enveloped me like a velvet, black mantle. I surrendered to his protective grasp, feeling like a child being comforted. Wind chimes seemed to dance in my ears and I fell asleep like that.

My sleep was shattered by the shrill screams of sirens, spinning blue lights and the babble of calling voices. Once more I was back in the ravine, my car, a red coffin, crinkled around me. The darkness was ripped open by floodlights!

"Here, over here," a husky male voice directed. "She's alive!"

My head pounded again and my leg throbbed in pain. The smell of damp earth and decomposed vegetation filled my nostrils. I was back where I'd started at the wreck site!

This time, when they wheeled me into the emergency room, the vines of machines were all too evident. IVs, monitors, respirators, all the trauma equipment was there as it should have been.

Mother was fluttering around outside of the swinging doors of the examining room. I could hear her voice. "Dear God! It's been five days! Why wasn't she found sooner? Will she live?" Her quiet sobbing I'd heard only once before when my father lay dead.

William's deep voice answered her in a low, indistinct, drone.

The trauma team ministered to my injuries, examining me from head to toes. X-Rays were taken, a cast applied to my hip and leg. Time dragged. They did a CT scan of my head. The final diagnosis was a severe concussion and a broken, right femur, and my hip broken. Some dehydration but, surprisingly, much less than they had expected. They seemed amazed that I had escaped going into shock!

My story of survival, over the five-day period, was heard and requested over and over. First by the state highway police, then by my excited mother, with a detached William standing by. Thirdly, I was questioned by my attending physician, and last of all I was required to repeat it several times for a therapist.

All of my story was dismissed as a hallucination experience caused by severe, untreated suffering, and trauma. I overheard Mother telling William that it was, "all because of her poor bruised brain."

William, in his best lawyer's voice, said, "Now, now, Virginia, Caroline is very sensible and practical. This is just part of the lifeline she invented in her mind to survive this tragedy. The mind can do amazing things to survive."

That's me. Good old, sensible, practical Caroline with her boring plans for her future life.

After several days and many hours of thought, I sent William back to Cleveland with my engagement ring in his pocket. I really believe that beneath his heartbroken demeanor, he was as relieved as I was that it was over between us.

Mother fluttered around as I prepared to leave the hospital to convalesce at her home in Florida.

Once in a while, on warm Gulf Coast nights, I walk on the white sand beach watching for a bright light in the sky and listening for the quiet whirring of an unseen engine. One of these days, perhaps I'll hear the song of wind chimes again, and feel my heart reaching for someone as dear to my dreams as Palu.

Secretly, I had kept the tiny, shining snippet of cloth they found clutched in my hand at the hospital.

They told me it was probably torn from the seat covers in my car, as I struggled to escape. A good explanation if my seat covers were a shimmering grey. But, they were tan leather!

SWEET STRANGER

OH, GOD! I wish the tape recorder in my head would stop—just cease, if only for a day. Just when my thoughts slow down, someone else steps up and pumps my hand while sing-songing to me about the last time they talked to Lillian.

"I was just talking to her in church last Sunday and she looked so well!" a neighbor informs me.

My eyes wander toward the casket with the blanket of red roses draped over the bottom half. Lillian's body is in it, I tell myself—your wife of thirty years. It pricks at my conscience, I search for my feelings, and I find only numbness.

"Yes, it was unexpected—her heart—yes, a heart attack." My arm is pumped some more, my back patted.

Lillian, her mouth petulant and demanding even in death, lies there in that last of all granted spaces, her black hair flecked with grey framing her pale face. I think of the many nuances of her face in flashes of anger and earnest concentration. Funny, I can't remember her ever crying or laughing, but I'm sure she did.

Walking into the viewing room, stepping softly, a tall man feels his solitary way through the crowded room approaching the coffin. He is a stranger to me. I watch as he walks toward the casket, his head bowed. He leans forward, placing a small nosegay of daisies close to her hand. Who is this person coming here and intruding on my grief? What right has he to gift my wife so tenderly in death?

I work my way toward the stranger, out of place here among familiar faces. He is gone, when I get to the viewing line, leaving me to wonder how he fit into Lillian's life, or when? Was it a brief encounter on a stair, or perhaps on the train to the city, where time sometimes hangs heavy on our hands and conversations with seatmates sometimes grow intimate over the clatter of the wheels on rails? The same railroad where I once had a brief encounter with the girl in the tiny, pillbox hat that was covered with pink, silk snapdragons. I'd been sitting in our small railroad station waiting for Lillian's train, the day before Lillian and I were to be married.

The girl sat across from me in the station. She sat on one of the old walnut benches, wearing a pale linen suit, her golden hair kissed her shoulders. She took my breath away! Our eyes met and held for seconds. Her sapphire eyes sparkled. Time seemed to stop for me. A train whistle screamed a train's arrival. She picked up her small bag. I followed, watching her board the train.

She hurried to a window seat as I stood on the platform watching. Her eyes sparkled wonderful messages to me as the train pulled out. I wanted to follow her.

Then I heard Lillian calling to me. "Here! I'm down here!" I looked toward the end of the station platform where Lillian stood waiting for me. "Didn't you see me?" she asked.

My feet felt like two heavy bricks as I crossed the platform to Lillian's side. "Hello dear," I mumbled lamely as she threw her arms around my neck. "I must have had a cinder in my eye to have missed seeing you."

That was a long time ago, but I've never forgotten the girl in the pink snapdragon hat.

Could it be that Lillian, too, had a brief encounter?... She never told me she liked daisies.

SIDESHOW

I KNOW I'll never forget my thirteenth birthday. A bright August morning promising another hot, Indiana day. Our farm looked dried out and tired.

Ma stood over the old coal stove, sizzling a few strips of fat bacon in a skillet, already wiping perspiration from her forehead with her apron.

"Teddy! Teddy! You get outta that bed and down here for breakfast." A thud sounded on the floor from overhead.

"Puhleeze, Ma, let me go to the carnival with Teddy. I've been savin' all year from my chore money so I can go."

Ma didn't answer me and I knew enough not to press too hard.

Teddy, my fifteen year old brother, dragged into the kitchen looking like he was still asleep. Eyes red, face swollen from sleep, but he was dressed to go into town in a fresh shirt and clean overalls. Sitting down at the old kitchen table, he began slurping the cornflakes Ma set in front of him.

"Ma." I tried again. "Teddy's goin' to the carnival, why can't I go too? After all this is my birthday..."

She turned from the stove, her face all thoughtful and the little worry lines showed between her eyes.

"Emma, if I let you go with Ted, will you promise me you'll not go near the sideshow? Ted, you'll watch after her?"

"Oh, yes! Yes, yes, Ma, I promise."

Teddy started burbling through a mouthful of cornflakes, "Why do I always have to drag Em along with me?" It was plain he wasn't pleased with the idea. "She's old enough to go with her own friends."

Ma just stood firm, her work roughened hands on her hips, waiting for him to answer yes or no.

"Oh, awright!" he finally answered.

I was so excited, I ran over and hugged him. He promptly shoved me away and kept stuffing his face.

It was Saturday, August 9th, 1934, and I thought it was going to be the best birthday I ever had.

Arthur France, Uncle Arthur, Ma's brother, was due at one o'clock in the afternoon to pick Ted and me up for the ride into Elgin. He lived on a neighboring farm, but spent a lot of time with us kids. Dad was away so much, working as a plumber on the side, to earn some extra dollars. I guess Uncle Arthur just felt kind of sorry for us or maybe it was because him and Aunt Annie didn't have any kids.

He took us in to Elgin just about every Saturday when he did their errands, usually dropping us at the movie house for the matinee. This day he drove his old truck to the fairgrounds entrance.

"You kids be here, right at this spot, at 4:30 sharp!" He waved and drove off, his old truck leaving a trail of blue smoke.

I loved the small town. It was so good to get away from the farm and the chores, and the greyness of the house. The carnival was ablaze in color...filled with sounds. The dreadful, breezeless afternoon left the colorful flags on top of the tents, hanging limp. Across the dusty field a calliope wailed.

Teddy walked ahead, his hands shoved deep into his baggy pants pockets. The good Lord only knows what he stores there.

I had to hurry my steps to keep up with him, he had such long legs. He had a very determined walk.

His red hair, so much like my own, curled in all directions and he needed a haircut. I was glad Ma could braid mine. Where Teddy took after Ma in being tall, I favored Pa's sister, small and bony.

Well, he led me straight to the Ferris wheel, the highest one I'd ever seen. The fellow running it took our tickets and after we sat, he fastened a safety bar across our laps. We clutched the bar and sat rigid as the big wheel slowly took us round-n-round. Breathless at the top, there were seconds when I wished I'd stayed home...then the ride was over, and we were set free by the operator. After that, I got a second wind. Of course, Ted acted unimpressed. He headed, straight off, for the sideshow tent!

"Ma said we weren't to go near the sideshow!"

"You didn't hear me promise, didja? She'll never know the difference if you don't tell her." He walked on toward the freak show, me slowly following.

"I don't know, Teddy..."

"Gimme' your quarter to get in."

"But, Teddy..."

"If yer goin' with me, you better give me yer money."

I kicked up dust with the toe of my shoe and held back. Ted's eyes were fierce with determination. Relenting, I pulled a knotted handkerchief from my dress pocket and unknotting it, I took a quarter from the small stack of coins it held. Teddy took the money and approached the ticket booth.

A man, the barker for the sideshow, rushed out of the tent, straw hat in hand, wiping sweat from the inside of the hatband with a grimy handkerchief. His black, curly hair bounced as he jumped up onto the platform. Dressed in a wild-plaid suit he used a small megaphone to call the crowd in.

Following the barker were four dark-haired, bedraggled looking women. Mr. Barker hailed their arrival, introducing them as "The Polynesian Beauties of the South Seas. "I wondered if they were real hula girls. They giggled and swayed. Their oversized hips were swathed in tattered looking grass skirts. The group moved in ragged rhythm to the plink of a ukulele strummed by a carnival roustabout. He wore a purple, crepe paper lei around his neck.

Teddy jabbed me in the ribs with his boney elbow, snickering behind his hands. A small group of about ten people gathered in the line to enter the tent. I noticed a sign over the entrance that read, "No one under 18 years will be admitted."

"We can't go in there." I whispered to Ted.

"Just keep quiet and keep walking." He pulled me along.

No one even looked at us funny. We were in. I can remember hearing the calliope in the background huffing out a rendition of "The Monkey Wrapped It's Tail Around the Flagpole."

Inside the sideshow tent several platforms were arranged in a circle. Each "stage" with a banner overhead advertising the attraction. The players in this strange, live exhibit waited their turn to start their own performances, one at a time.

Teddy kept pushing me along toward the front of the crowd.

The dreary tent was very hot and smelled of human sweat. I hated it!

On the first platform, a person billed as "Half Man/Half Woman" sat on a stool explaining his/her condition. Teddy's eyes were bugged, and I couldn't understand a word the person said. Then, the man/woman, who wore lipstick and sported a black beard, offered to show the "intimate proof" of his/her mixed gender, for an additional quarter...in the back room. Teddy pulled me away in a hurry.

At the next platform, a woman sat on a colorful Indian blanket. She had large brown eyes with long lashes and red hair, exactly the color of mine, cut in a close bob. But her poor legs were cruelly deformed, withered and gnarled. She had no arms! A banner overhead announced "Aurora, The Miracle Woman."

As I looked at her I remembered Ma saying, "Never make fun...remember, 'There but for the grace of God go I.'" I thought to myself that the great Creator must have decided to grace her with one perfect gift, her feet. Her feet were supple, well-formed, and, I came to find out, educated!

I felt a revulsion in the pit of my stomach. I didn't want to look at Aurora but felt held there. Her melodious voice spread over the group. Eyes held aloof, she didn't really look at anyone. "Ladies and Gentlemen, step in closer and I will show you that with determination anyone can overcome almost any disability."

I didn't want to move closer but the people shoved me.

Fright had made my feet like lead.

She picked up an embroidery hoop with her left foot and carefully took out an already threaded needle from the work on the hoop. She did it all so fast and easy-like, holding the hoop with her left foot, the needle between her toes of her right foot.

She continued to talk, "Never think for one minute that I do not have a rich rewarding life." Laying the needlework down, Aurora reached for a cigar box lying near her. Opening it with her toes, she took out a photograph. Holding it up with her foot, she said, "This is my son, born to me and my husband ten years ago." A handsome, young boy's face smiled from the photo.

Once again, I felt sickness in the bottom of my stomach.

The air stunk. It was so hot...yet I shivered, wishing Teddy would take me out of there. Salty bile started to rise in my throat. I felt the sweat running down from my temples. Quickly, I worked my way through the crowd and headed for a flap I saw in the tent. I pulled it open, hoping for some cooler air.

Instead, hot air seemed to hit me in the face. Stepping out of the tent, I failed to see one of the ropes that held the tent up. I fell over it, sprawling headfirst into the dry-dirt field, in the rear of the tent rows.

Struggling to get back on my feet, I was suddenly blinded by a burlap-type sack being pulled over my head. I threw up my hands trying to free myself. It smelled of filth and chickens. Two strong arms pinned me to the ground. Dust clogged my nose and mouth. I fought with all my might, scarcely able to breathe.

I pulled myself to my feet only to he knocked down again!

It seemed like the most important thing on my mind at that point was to stay on my feet. He knocked me down again and again. I kept trying to crawl to my feet, pleading with my tormentor, praying out loud to God. I knew the demon was a man...no woman could have such strength or smell that bad.

If only I could have screamed. I was never able to scream.

Even in the midst of the savage attack, it seemed unreal that I could hear that calliope wheezing out a raucous circus tune from across the field.

Reality almost left me, my head throbbed, my eyes burned.

I was no longer sure of my location. But, I could just make out a low hum of voices nearby.

Finally, I heard my attacker's voice, low and guttural, as he talked to himself. He struck me in the stomach. I went down on my face. I felt his weight holding me down as he sat on my back. "If I can reach a rock I'll hit her in the head with it!" He fumbled around. Then, "I'll get her shoe off and hit her in the head with the heel."

Pure instinct told me to curl my toes in my leather sandals.

The shoes wouldn't come off. Once more and finally, I struggled to my feet, the sack still over my face. A blow to my abdomen forced me to my knees and darkness!

The next thing I remember was someone pulling the bag off of my face and seeing Aurora, seated in a wheel chair, being pushed by the barker, busting through the tent flap in a flurry of dust. The demon had escaped. Aurora's eyes were wild and full of fear. The cripple was, nevertheless, in command... screaming orders at the man with the curly black hair.

"Is she dead? Oh, God! Joe, see to her."

He bent over me feeling my neck. As he did, I tried to speak. All that came out was a low moan.

"She's coming around," Joe reported. "Looks pretty good in the eyes but she's taken a bad beating."

Aurora yelled at two roustabouts standing nearby. "Put the child in my tent." They moved quickly at her command. To Joe, she said, "Get the deputy sheriff. He's on the grounds."

The barker leaned over and picked up the gunny sack that had been over my head. He slammed it down by Aurora's wheelchair with obvious disgust. The movement was not lost on the woman and their eyes met for a brief second, as if sharing knowledge.

Settled on a cot inside Aurora's tent, I was almost beyond caring about much of anything, I hurt so bad and was so tired. Teddy broke into the group that surrounded me. "Emma! Emma! What happened? Oh, my God, Em! Talk to me." He knelt by my side and started to cry.

"Take me home, Teddy." I whispered and then, it was like something broke, and I cried all the tears in the world.

The carny who played the ukulele took over as Aurora's helper when Joe left to find the sheriff. He pushed her into the tent up close to me. I stared up at her trying not to show my feelings of helplessness.

"You OK, kid? Now don't be scared anymore, you're goin' to be fine. We'll get you home to your folks just as soon as possible."

I could only sniffle and cling to Teddy's hand.

There was a sound of voices at the tent entrance and Joe came in with the deputy sheriff, Jim Staff.

"OK, OK. What's the trouble?"

"We have a little girl here who was beat up pretty bad."

Staff asked, "Who's this kid here?" He pointed at Teddy.

"I'm her brother."

Officer Staff bent over me, not touching me, as he inspected my bruised face. "Have you called in a doctor to examine the girl yet?"

"We haven't had time to call a doctor yet or ask the child any questions." Aurora answered him. "But, if you want to get at specifics, why don't you let me talk to her first...in private? You know..." She gave Staff a knowing look. He hesitated just a moment then hustled everyone out, leaving me and Aurora alone. She wheeled her chair close to me.

"Now, kid it's very important that you tell me if you can identify who did this to you. Can you?"

I shook my head no.

"OK, then. Was there anything about him you can tell me?"

I whispered, "Yes."

Can you remember...was it a man?

I started to cry again and nodded my head. "He spoke funny...mean...foreign..."

"Good, now Emma, that is your name? Now, Emma, this is very, very important. Did that guy who beat you do anything else to you?" I felt my face burn red with embarrassment. "I know this is tough, kid, but you can talk to me."

"No, he just hit me with his fists...I stayed on my feet as long as I could."

"That's a smart girl. You just rest here a little while and we'll get this all over with as soon as we can and get you home."

There was a commotion outside the tent and Uncle Arthur shoved his way in past everyone. He swept me into his arms. I cried harder than ever. "Now, now, you're going to be fine." I never knew I could be so glad to see anyone. "Oh, Uncle Arthur, Uncle Arthur..." I repeated it over and over.

Aurora sat quietly in the big, cumbersome wheelchair. "How do you do, Mr. France. Your little niece will be fine in a couple of days. No real harm done. Would you be so kind as to wheel me outside so we can talk?"

Uncle Arthur stepped away from me in a startled way. I thought he was just shocked by Aurora's appearance. He pushed her chair outside, almost like he'd done it a hundred times. I could hear them.

Aurora- "It's been a long time, Arthur."

Arthur- "So, Ada was right when she said that you'd choose this life!"

Aurora- "Dear brother, Arthur, what other life could there have ever been for me?"

Arthur- "Aw, Aurora, we loved, you—all of us—Ma never did get over it when you left with that stranger."

Aurora- "I had one chance for a life of my own and I took it. I have never forgotten you all, but this is my life now, with this show. I belong somewhere now. In fact, this is my sideshow! I own it lock, stock and freaks! These people depend on me."

Arthur- "Are you going to try and see Ada? After all she is your sister."

Aurora- "No reunions for me, brother dear. I'm just glad fate allowed us these few minutes...I hate it that it's under these circumstances. I'm glad that I got to see Ada's kids. They'll get over this. Anyway, I was always an embarrassment to Ada. Don't tell her or the kids that I was here. Do that for me and I'll see that we don't book within a hundred miles of here again."

Arthur- "We love you, dear sister." A choke in his voice.

The calliope continued in its unrelenting arias; the sound wafted across the carnival lot as Uncle Arthur drove the old truck toward home. Ted and I huddled in the back seat.

"Ma's going to be real mad at us when we get home." Ted nodded his head. "I wish I'd never heard of a carnival," he grumbled.

The sheriff never was able to find out who had attacked me. But, two weeks later, there was an item in the *Elgin News* stating that a sideshow geek, named Brutus Cootman, was found dead, hanging under a railroad culvert near Elgin. It seemed that he had accidentally slipped off the bridge above and hung himself. A burlap sack he was carrying on his shoulder got caught on a railroad tie when he fell, strangling him. He'd been dead for several days before the body was found and identified by former carnival workers.

DO NOT DISTURB

THE INTERCOM buzzed on my desk; I pushed the button and answered. "Yes, Mr. Bower?"

"Miss Yates! Come in here, please." The gravelly voice of Jason Bower, my boss, reverberated around my ears. I, involuntarily, jerked my ear away from the phone. Mr. Bower always used the intercom or telephone as though it were a hollow tube and he was five hundred miles away from the person on the other end. My ears rang. "Oh! Uh, uh...," he continued to bluster, "never mind, just come in here."

I scrambled from my chair and headed for his office door.

Ever since he had quit smoking those big black, smelly cigars, Mr. Bower had been acting peculiar. His office door was always closed, and he insisted everyone must knock before entering. Before the cigars went, he didn't care who went in or when. He was always jovial, his florid complexion changing shades of red with his moods, which were varied and pleasant. All of that had changed. His manner now was steadier...disagreeable *all* the time. The usual large-toothed smile had been replaced with a grim taciturn demeanor.

Standing in front of him I said, "What can I do for you, Mr. Bower?"

He grunted a sort of greeting to me from where he sat behind his massive desk. He fidgeted with a pile of correspondence. His round, pudgy body was stuffed into a grey and white tweed suit, size 46 short. His narrow black tie was an exclamation mark on a stiff white shirt. He wore his grey-white hair cropped into even spikes on his round dome of a head, reminding me, somehow, of a porcupine all hunched up and mad.

"Just a minute. Just a minute," he bumbled, running his hands nervously over the brush-bristle hair. That's one thing that intrigued me about the man, his hands. They were small and almost delicate. Not the hands of a former machinist turned engineer. But, he was that, a first-rate civil engineer.

He got up from behind his desk leaving me standing, waiting, as he thumped toward a filing cabinet with that flat-footed gait some fat men have. His complexion seemed somewhat more colorful than usual as he jerked a file drawer open, and pulled out a box of mint-flavored toothpicks. Since the cigars had been relinquished, toothpicks had taken their place in his mouth. He chewed on them all day.

Reseating himself at his desk, he informed me that he'd be out of town for three days, then went through the ceremony of the keys. "The keys to my desk are in the top filing drawer. Use them at your discretion." With a nod of his head, I was dismissed. "Close the door going out," he mumbled.

Sitting at my desk that same afternoon, I thought about Mr. Bower and his metamorphosis since he hired me two years ago. The gentle, devoted family man had gone through life finding only the best in everyone. This Santa Claus of a man was a mere shadow of the undefined lump who now hid behind the big oak desk in the inner office, daring anyone to enter.

Two days after he left on the business trip I found it necessary to unlock his desk for certain papers I needed. It was then that I solved the riddle of Mr. Bower's dire need for privacy. In the large bottom drawer of his desk, I found a partially knitted, red wool sweater of enormous proportions and two knitting needles. Hidden under the excess yarn was a fine Cuban cigar, still wrapped and ringed.

Somehow, I had the feeling that when the sweater was completed, the cigar would be smoked! With new office rules, that would mean he would be smoking it outside if he lit up.

I teetered on the edge of sincere hope for the smoker's recovery, and a wish that the real Mr. Bower would stand up and be counted, with that big ugly cigar clenched firmly in his big toothy smile, and the office door open again.

CARRIE

EVERYONE in town knew about Crazy Carrie. They were used to seeing her shuffling around in the old railroad station at the end of Main Street. Most evenings at dusk, she'd appear in the small gabled station with its church-like spire, always carrying a big brown grocery bag.

In the bag was an old, ragged Indian blanket, a few bits of food, some scraps of paper, and a small sewing basket.

These were all that remained, to remind anyone of the wife and seamstress she had once been. All that was left of that former lady was a mumbling, bent old woman dressed in castoff clothes.

Charley Closser, the pharmacist, who had known Carrie from girlhood, was the only person in town Carrie would talk to.

"Some looker she was!" Charley would comment. "Yes, siree! Her auburn curls flashin' in the sun... her smilin' green eyes always ready to laugh. Married Tommy Blake. My, how she loved that man! He was good lookin' too, I guess. Anyways, the women sure liked him. He was the station master at the old railroad station."

Charley, the pharmacist, was the one who sort of watched out for Carrie and her comings an' goings. Charley'd never married and some old timers around town said that was because he'd been in love with Carrie once himself!

If you asked Charley what made her the way she was, he'd tell you it was "on account of Tommy's murder." Someone put a bullet in Tommy's head right there in the old station on a summer afternoon long ago.

"No one could understand why anyone would shoot Tommy Blake," Charley'd say. "Well, Carrie never got over it. The sheriff back then was Kendall Hatch. He just sort of wrote it off to a robbery gone wrong, 'cause no money was missing."

Charley's eyes always got teary at about this point in the story. "Carrie got strange then and started her station vigils, mumblin' all the time that she knew who done it! No one paid much attention to her talk and figured if she wanted to sleep in the old station it wouldn't hurt anything." That was about all the little pharmacist knew.

About thirty years after the killing, Ex-Sheriff Hatch died. Carrie became extremely agitated then, and nothing would soothe her. Charley thought she was just sensitive to the old sheriff's death.

The Hatch family started to assemble from far and near for the funeral. Then one night Carrie was sleeping on the same old bench she always slept on in the station. When the eleven o'clock Flyer stopped, Cloris Hatch, the sheriff's sister, disembarked. She was the schoolmarm who'd left town just about the same time as Tommy's murder. She stepped into the dreary station and headed for the street.

When the early morning light brought people into the depot, a terrible sight greeted their eyes. Cloris Hatch was lying on the floor in a pool of her own blood, a surprised expression on her face. A pair of tailor's scissors sticking out of her chest! She was very dead.

Carrie was curled up on the old bench, her Indian blanket covering her snugly. She hugged one wrinkled old hand to her heart and a peaceful smile was on her face. She, too, was dead!

The police officer who came found a piece of old notepaper clutched in Carrie's hand. Unfolding the yellowed, old paper, he held it up and read it. "I'll be at the station at 3:30 p.m. This can't go on. It's either her or me!" It was dated the same day that Tommy Blake was shot, and it was signed, "Cloris."

RUNAWAY

I REMEMBER the big wooden cabinet that stood in the entrance hall of my grandmother's house. I could just reach the handle that hung on the side of it. Not more than five or six years of age, I found the machine to be mystical.

Already aware that it had to be wound up before it would work, I'd wind it, then lift the lid and place the arm holding the wooden needle on the record that whirled like a dervish. Then I'd stand with my ears cocked toward the slots where the sound came out. Music would swell out and around my head. My excitement would escalate. People singing, a piano playing, a drum rattling in the background left me with wonder in my childish heart. I'd think very hard about how those people, those voices, got into that box and sang that music to me. Oh! How I wanted to see them.

Of course, it wasn't very long before the secret of the phonograph became clear to me. Then I wasn't sure but that my earlier fantasy, of the people being in the box, wasn't more fun. But, I was always curiosity driven.

Grandma would chuckle at my queries. "Curiosity killed the cat!" she'd tell me. Well, I wasn't sure about it killing any cats, but it certainly helped to inhibit my freedom.

You see, they thought that I enjoyed running away, Mama, Daddy, and Grandma, because I seemed to wander off a lot. But it wasn't that.

What it was, was that I could see so much beauty all around me, especially where the dogwood bloomed in the small forest down the road. I would walk there picking up pieces of jewel-like glass that sparkled in the sun like rubies or emeralds. The footpath was a bonanza of unmined jewels. I knew in my deepest heart that it was broken glass bottles left there long ago by some strangers, but the woods transported me to a different place, I guess... Of course, I couldn't analyze it then, or tell Mama why I was compelled to wander a quarter of a mile from home to my own place in the world.

That's how my curiosity got me tied by my waist, with a long rope, attached to Grandma's big apple tree. I wanted to tell them, "I'm not running away when I go off. I'm running to what calls me!" They wouldn't have understood any more than I did then.

My, I do get winded easily of late. The sun is warm and I'll just sit awhile before I walk another path here in the woods.

"Jenny! Jenny! You wake up! You've had us hunting for you for hours."

I open my purse for them to see the pieces of pretty glass I've found. "See, aren't these pretty?"

"Come on old girl. There'll be no more solo walks for you after I speak to your doctor about this escapade! Get her into the car," the woman in the nurse's uniform ordered the man standing by the station wagon. On the door of the wagon was painted, "Lotus Glen Retirement Village."

"I wasn't running away. You won't tie me to the tree, will you, Mama?"

THE MECHANICAL MAN

FRANK STEIN, at age thirty, was a young man who was always fast on his feet going nowhere.

A brown-bagger at lunch time, Frank headed for his favorite green metal bench in the mall where he worked as an assistant manager of a shoe store.

He chomped on his usual bologna sandwich while listening to the hum of the mall's heart. The chatter and the fuss, the squeals of the children, the language of the passers-by all blended in with the changing faces of the daily crowd.

Frank liked the mall. On November 20th, there was an extra bit of excitement for him to observe. The Digby-Hones Department Store, straight across the mall walkway from his chosen bench, was the focus of a new promotional show due to start that day.

A banner over the air-shield entranceway announced: "SEE THE MECHANICAL MAN AND SNOWFLOWER, THE LIVING DOLL. SHOWS AT 12:00 Noon and 7:00 P.M. in our front window."

Picking up his bag of trash, Frank tossed it into a nearby receptacle. Slowly, he walked across the aisle, dodging people who were waiting for the show to start.

The crackle of the sound system caught the attention of the gathering crowd.

"What's this all about?" someone whispered.

"Oh, you know, one of those quirky mechanical man shows. They're all fakey!"

Frank's pale blue eyes wandered over the window set. Heavy blue curtains were hung professionally to make a doorway through which the performers could enter and exit the window space.

Checking his watch, the shoe salesman uttered a couple of mild expletives under his breath. He'd have to miss the new show that day or be late back at the Active Footwear Store.

He felt he had to set a good example for the other employees.

His motto was, "The customer is always right," (even if their feet stink).

Stein had an Ichabod Crane kind of body—all long bones and big joints. He had a friendly Jim Carrey face. Other than mall sitting, his passion in life was collecting baseball cards.

As the shoe store assistant manager, he was reasonably happy. As a complete person, he yearned for a soul mate. His long back, bent over a pair of slim, lovely legs in the shoe store, was about as close as he ever got to meeting his dream lover.

Hurrying back to work, he made a mental note to take his lunchtime later the next day to ensure he'd be present at the Digby-Hones show.

"Hey, Frankie boy! What's going on?"

Frank jumped in his skin and stopped.

"Nothing much." He wished Jake Turner would disappear. Jake had been heckling Frank since they were both in the eighth grade. He really got off on putting Frank down. A born bully.

"Heard yer cousin Sherry's getting hitched to some foreigner," Jake persisted.

"Naw, she's marrying a truck driver from Boise."

"That's what I said...a foreigner."

"Nothin' foreign about him I can see," Frank muttered.

Oh, crap! Frank thought. Here come the digs at my manhood next. A small jagged scar near the corner of his left eye turned bright red. A sure sign that the shoe salesman was getting upset. Turning fast on his feet, he mumbled, "Due back at the store."

He fled the abrasive Turner, leaving him with his big mouth open and a new insult forming there.

Frank's home life was quiet and dull. He lived with his mother whose main interest in life was pursuing her family's and friends' business and feeding Frank greasy, though kosher, meals. Her name was Abby. Frank's father had been dead for many years, an early victim of high cholesterol. The father-son relationship had never been close.

"Don't forget to take the trash out, son. I'm going over to your Aunt Esther's for a little visit tonight."

Delighted to be left to his own devices, the relief showed on his face. Abby didn't notice. At least she wouldn't chatter through the whole evening, screwing up his concentration, while he sorted out his favorite baseball cards.

If Abby ever felt any rejection from Frank, she never let on. Secretly, she always felt inadequate as a mother—even more so, since he had grown to adulthood.

Lunchtime the next day saw Frank Stein, brown bag in hand, hurrying toward the green bench a half hour earlier than usual. He gulped his lunch down, keeping an eye on Digby-Hones's front window.

The window was empty except for the heavy blue curtain that was draped to serve as an entryway for the performers.

Music, a lively Dixieland melody, blared from the loud speakers. A figure stood in the entranceway between the curtains. It was a man.

He was slightly built, dressed in a brightly colored plaid suit, red bow tie, white gloves, black shoes, and white spats. On his head, jauntily set, was a straight brimmed, natural straw hat. His face was painted with clown-like precision; his black shoes shined like mirrors. Brown eyes were fixed in a perpetual stare.

As the music rose, the mechanical man bowed from the waist, doffing his hat and replacing it on his round, bald head. Every movement seemed to be propelled by an unseen motor. On his back was a big wind-up key which turned slowly as he performed, making the audience laugh. He was good! Very, very good.

The audience applauded loudly as he finished his act and exited the window.

Frank watched, unable to take his eyes off the performer. The music ebbed and the blue curtain closed. The shoe salesman was awed by what he had seen.

Music crackled from the speakers again. This time it was "The Wedding of the Painted Doll." A disconnected voice invited the crowd to, "Stay where you are everybody. Digby-Hones proudly presents Snowflower, the only, truly life-sized doll in the world! We invite you to come in and visit our toy center on the second floor for the premiere performance of this moving, speaking marvel of a doll. The show will start in fifteen minutes."

The co-owners of the show were two ex-circus dwarfs, André and Gunther. They had been given dressing rooms in the rear of the stockroom section of the store, an area rarely used by any of the employees. Closeted there, their heads together over a small table, they discussed the crisis that could force them out of business.

The Mechanical Man

"I'm telling you, Gunther, that Leonard ain't kiddin' around this time. He told me that a chicken farm was beginning to look pretty good to him!"

"He's just tryin' to heist you for more money," Gunther said.

"No. I don't think so. We finally got out of those sleazy sideshows and I ain't about to let ole Leonard Higgins put us back there!"

Leonard Higgins had been their main attraction since they went on the road together. He was sixty-seven years old, and getting tired of the traveling. The rigors of the mechanical act were getting to his old joints.

He loved to goad the dwarfs with not-so-veiled threats of leaving them. He especially liked to irritate André, whom he really disliked.

What to do about Leonard became the dwarfs' second most time consuming problem to talk about. The dwarfs' first concern was always, Snowflower.

André leaned toward Gunther at the table. "We gotta replace the old man. You know that and I know that."

"Geez, André, can't we put an ad in the paper?"

André socked Gunther, not too softly, in the head. "No way! Are you nuts? We can't allow the old man to run around loose knowing we're going to get rid of him, 'specially when he's drunk and can talk too much about Snowflower."

Gunther nodded his head in agreement.

The dwarfs were very near the same size, about four feet tall. André, "The Mouth," as Leonard liked to refer to him, was a bit heavier than Gunther, with a dark complexion and almost black eyes. His hair stood up in short, scared-looking tufts on his over-sized head.

Gunther, blond with pale blue eyes and full lips, reminded one of an albino bullfrog hopping around at André's bidding.

"No one must know the truth about Snowflower," he echoed his fellow dwarf.

"I'm glad you understand, Gunther. It could mean the end of the show. The end of our livelihood. They could even take the doll away from us!"

Leonard was laid out in his dressing room, a bottle of bourbon resting amiably in one fine-boned hand. He upended the bottle pouring the liquid down his throat, his face reflecting the pleasure of the firewater's journey to his stomach.

"A little bracer is what I needed." He talked out loud to himself. "They can't appreciate what it takes out of me to give that kind of a performance. They never understand that I'm an artist." With the paint still on his face, he stripped off the plaid suit and removed the spats and shoes.

"The little bastards are starting to get nervous about ole Leonard." He sat down abruptly on the old broken down cot that served as a bed and a chair. "Ole Leonard ain't givin' in to them," he said to his sad-clown reflection in the wall mirror. "No siree! Got more than one ace up my sleeve." He giggled as the booze started to take effect.

The old performer was tired of the bickering that went on between the dwarfs, not to mention the annoying presence of that airhead girl they'd picked up somewhere.

"Everything's about our darling, Snowflower. That's all I hear is Snowflower. Her wardrobe, her hair. Her miserable acting as a doll. Some doll!" A retard, if you asked him.

"André tells her what to do, how to look at the crowd, how to move, and how to smile at the people so she'll show those incredibly white teeth. Never allowing anyone near her, and those perfect tits hangin' out of the top of her costumes, just enough to entice. Snowflower! Beautiful, innocent, untouchable Snowflower! BAH!"

André pounded on Leonard's dressing room door.

"Leonard! You in there?" His small hands were sweating. They always did when he was nervous.

The door opened revealing Higgins in his underwear, still wearing the face paint. Leonard's bald head shone under the one electric bulb that was lit in the center of the ceiling. Red-rimmed eyes protruded under ugly fatty pouches above and under his eyes. Their color lost in time and liquor.

"Well, well, if it ain't the mouth! Where's yer little pale shadow that goes in and out with you?" He laughed at his own joke. "And what can be the use of him is more than I can see." Another laugh. Mockingly, he bowed low over the threshold.

"Me and Gunther have been thinking about what you've been saying about retiring. We thought, maybe, you'd stay with us as a front man for a while...at least until you've helped us train a replacement. Then we'll buy your contract up and pay you for an extra year...sort of a bonus. How does that sound to you?"

"You serious? Hell! That ain't no good deal at all. If I stay, I get my money anyhow. I'm not gonna train any rube, then just fade into the sunset. After all, this is an art we're talking about here." Leonard's bloodshot eyes danced with glee as he tormented André.

"We're prepared to pay you well if you'll go along. I'm sure we can settle on a price. How about it?"

While Leonard stood there enjoying his position of power, for a change, Gunther came running full speed down the dark hall. Gasping for breath, his eyes rolling in his big head, he blurted out to André, "Come quick! Gawd, André, I can't find her. I've looked everywhere."

"What do you mean, you can't find her? Weren't you watching her?" André started running down the hallway from where Gunther had just come. "C'mon. Where was the last place you saw her?"

He forgot about Leonard who stood transfixed watching the two dwarfs panic. Instead of following, he turned his back and opened another bottle of liquor.

Gunther, stomping his feet, was hitting himself in the head with both fists. "I made her comfortable in the dressing room just after the noon show. I musta forgot something."

By this time, André was halfway down the corridor approaching the stairway to the roof. Climbing to the roof exit door the dwarfs pushed at the steel door with all their might. Rusty hinges finally gave way stubbornly and very slowly. Surely, André thought, Snowflower couldn't have opened the door herself!

The roof was a mélange of broken light bulbs, pieces of wire, metal containers and even an old picnic table—probably a relic of some long-forgotten window display.

Snowflower stood at the very edge of the roof looking skyward. Her right arm held high, reaching for the sun.

"Oh, damn, damn, damn!" André yelled. "The signal. The signal. She's sending the signal!" In unison, both dwarfs leaped for Snowflower and pulled her away from the edge of the roof to safety.

The two insignificant circus clowns thought they had hit it rich when they found Leonard Higgins drinking his life away in a cheap, run-down sideshow. They plotted a course for themselves, using Higgins and making themselves owners of the show.

That led them all on a cross-country tour, performing at upgraded malls that had paid them well. Although Leonard refused to believe it, Snowflower's appearance with the bizarre group made them all richer.

Snowflower was their living doll with the allure of a Pied Piper. The people, particularly the children, couldn't resist her, dressed like an Indian princess, in a soft, pink chamois Indian dress. Her long silky hair, shining golden, hung to her waist. Black doe-eyes peeked out from behind a fringe of shimmering bangs. She was exactly four feet tall, perfectly proportioned. Her pink rose-tinged skin was unblemished, her small mouth made a little pout.

A very special attraction, she lured the crowds into the toy departments of expensive stores where they performed.

André and Gunther were never able to understand how they could have been so fortunate as to have discovered the remarkable creature. Like "Jack and the Beanstalk," they were afraid they would awaken a sleeping giant one day. One who would claim her away from them. Never, never, they swore to each other on their respective mother's names, would they reveal to anyone how they found her.

The story of their find was, however, the main source of their most intimate conversations with each other. They loved to relive that night.

It was only a few weeks ago that Gunther waited in their RV for André to finish the last minute packing after a show. "Gawd, it's cold tonight." André yelled at Gunther, who was slouched behind the steering wheel. "Can't you come out here and help me a little."

Gunther was sound asleep.

"That lush, Leonard, took off without helping at all. C'mon. Get off yer ass and help with the job here."

Gunther never moved.

As André worked, he heard a high-pitched sound that seemed to come from the hill directly behind the RV. As he listened, the sound shifted tones. High then low. Then the pitch would swing in range. The dwarf could see his breath in the faint light.

It was 2:00 a.m. Clouds partially covered a cold moon. The dwarf shuddered a bit in the darkness. Still intrigued by the sound, he walked a short distance up the hill.

"Gawd-dammit," he muttered as he stumbled over something he couldn't quite see. Flicking his cigar lighter he searched the spot where he stumbled. There on the ground was the body of a girl. He felt like running, but instead reached down to feel her neck for a pulse. He couldn't feel any.

"Oh, Jesus!" He cried out getting ready to run from the body, when she moved. She threw an arm up into the air, like a drowning person.

"Are you alive?" André felt stupid as hell asking such a question. But to his amazement, she answered.

"I am damaged. Incapacitated."

"Where are you hurt?" Another stupid question. "Can I get you some help?"

"Perhaps you can help me yourself."

Here I am, thought André, an insignificant clown being asked by the most beautiful girl I've ever seen, if I will help her. "I'll do what I can, but first I must get a better light to see you." He turned away quickly. "I'll be right back."

He ran stumbling back to the truck screaming at Gunther to wake up. "Get up you lazy lout! We have work to do. Quick! Quick!"

"Aw, shit, André, I've been bustin' my ass all day."

"C'mon, c'mon, I found a girl up there on the hill. She's in trouble and we have to help her."

"Sounds like a lot more then trouble to me. Who is she?"

The Mechanical Man

"Only the most beautiful creature I've ever seen!"

"Now, I know you're crazy."

The dwarfs, flashlights in hand, climbed the forested hill, not knowing that their lives would never be the same again.

Lifting the girl gently, the two men carried her down the hill to their motor home. They placed her on a bed.

"Different looking kind of girl," Gunther commented.

The girl's eyes never left his face.

"Who are you? What's your name?" Gunther asked her.

"I am known as Number 25. I'm a helper."

"She must be delirious." André offered.

The dwarfs stood looking at the strange person they had rescued, not knowing what to do next.

"Where are you hurt?" Gunther found his tongue again.

"My right arm seems to be short circuited, and a fracture exists in the circuit panel of my controller, making it difficult for me to move."

The dwarfs just stood there feeling foolish and embarrassed.

"We ain't experts on circuitry an' probably can't do much to help..." André's voice trailed off, he blinked wildly at Gunther who was stupefied.

"I will tell you what to do, but you must listen carefully to my instructions. You will need some special micro-tools. They are stored in the lower part of my back. You will find a small structured opening like a tiny door. Open it and remove the packet of tools you'll find there.

Gunther thought he was going to pass out. His eyes bulged more as he paled. His heart pounded. Running away seemed like a good idea for a moment.

André, cigar butt clenched between his teeth, found it hard to breathe. "C'mere!" He reached out and grabbed Gunther by the collar pulling him toward the far end of the RV.

"You listen to me. We're going to do exactly what she says. You keep your cool an' let me handle this." Gunther was sweating and his big eyes bulged. He nodded his assent, unable to speak.

They laid the girl's body over the table in the RV. Word by word, they did what she told them to do to fix what was wrong with her.

"Look, she's moving!" Gunther watched the girl ...or whatever she was, stand up on her feet. She was about the same height as he was. Her yellow hair hung in a braid past her tiny waist. She was dressed in a blue, metallic jumpsuit.

Her skin was the color of peaches. Moving toward the door, she said, "I must get to the top of the hill. I must signal them."

"Who, who?" Gunther asked.

"Shut up! You sound like an owl." André punched Gunther in the head again. "Wait, wait!" André yelled after the girl. "You can't go out there wandering around by yourself. It ain't safe. Someone could harm you."

"Harm me? Why would anyone harm me?"

"There are lots of humans out there who wouldn't understand how valuable, er, important you are. They might not understand you being here."

"I must send a signal." She moved forward intently.

"We'll go with you to protect you," Andre offered.

The dwarfs weren't quite sure about the signal sending, but 25 seemed so set on it that they went along. Reaching the peak of the hill, she stood very still with her right hand held high above her head, taking the position in all four directions.

Gunther and André were unable to discern any sound. They were both shivering in the cold night air. Moving around to keep warm, they waited for two hours as 25 repeated her movements, over and over. Talking softly to each other, they speculated on the possibility that they were in the presence of a space-type creature. An idea they had great difficulty accepting. After two hours, the sky was getting light.

"Please, Miss, we must go now and you should come along."

She responded to the order following the two men down the hill, back to the motor home. Once inside they seated her again. André watched her closely.

The drive toward their home destination in Ohio was uneventful. The problem of controlling the valuable personage from space (if that was the case) baffled them.

If she were to be discovered by anyone, they would be subjected to a media frenzy and would probably lose her completely. That was unthinkable, for already a plan had formed to include her in their act with Leonard. It would be a presentation that would make them all rich!

During the trip to Ohio, they conceived the idea of how to control Number 25. They started referring to it as "making her comfortable. "Disconnecting her mobility circuitry did the trick. Making her unable to walk assured them of some free time to pursue their other duties.

During the journey, they named her Snowflower.

For reasons he couldn't understand himself, Frank Stein grew more and more engrossed in the daily performance of the mechanical man. He extended his lunch hour each day to enable him to see all of Leonard's act.

Obsessed with the mechanizations of Leonard's neck and limbs, Frank even went to the public library and studied books on kinetics. His body seemed to be perfectly suited to the task, growing ever more proficient at the art of appearing to be mechanical.

Abby, Frank's mother, became aware that a new interest gripped her son. In some small way she welcomed his having broader interests. Beyond that, she paid little attention to his comings and goings. Although it was true that she loved Frank very much, she never admitted to anyone her disappointment in her son. The fact was, she felt he would never excel at much of anything. If he had been from her husband Irving's loins, she would muse to herself, he would have been something!

But, she and her husband had kept secret the fact that Frank was a foundling. He'd been left on the doorstep of their young Rabbi Berensen, some thirty years before. The Rabbi had quietly arranged for the childless Steins to adopt the child.

The day Frank visited the toy department at Digby-Hones to see Snowflower was to become the most important, exciting day of his life.

The stage was far larger than the display window, and a dark blue, lamé curtain shimmered under the lights. Music started to play over the sound system, a lively march. The curtain parted and the two dwarf clowns swept across the stage rolling, somersaulting, and spinning on their small feet. The clown costumes they wore were brilliant red, purple, and yellow. The children squealed with delight. As the music hit a crescendo, the curtain parted again revealing Leonard dressed in the costume of a toy soldier. He stood very straight, stiffly holding onto a wooden gun that was held over his shoulder. His face was painted in bright colors.

The Mechanical Man

The sound system bellowed, "Ladies, gentlemen and children, Digby-Hones takes great pleasure in presenting one of the world's most accomplished mechanical men." The crowd applauded. Leonard marched and drilled in perfect time to the music, ending his routine with a stiff military salute to the audience. They loved it. Frank was dazzled.

A drum roll sent the small clowns back to center stage, where they bowed in mock reverence toward the slowly opening curtain in the back. A hum came up from the crowd watching. Standing in the pin-spotlight was Snowflower, her golden hair gleaming in the light. She was dressed in a turquoise, chamois-skin Indian dress that reached just below her thighs, revealing her lovely legs. Her small feet were encased in soft, ankle-high deerskin boots, the exact color of her dress. The same color was picked up in the streamers of ribbons that trailed down her hair in the back.

The shoe salesman gasped a little and sat transfixed.

He thought Snowflower was the most beautiful creature he had ever seen.

She danced slowly around the stage, twirling herself in time to an Indian drum which was the only accompaniment. Her large doe-eyes were fixed on the audience, a sweet smile on her pink lips. Then she stopped in front of a standing microphone and began to talk in that strange sing-song manner she had of speaking.

"My name is Snowflower. I come from a different place and time. I am four feet tall and weigh sixty pounds. My friends, the clowns, have brought me here to see you, and for you to see me. Thank you all."

"Jesus!" André whispered, "She got through that okay. Now hold your breath, the song is next."

Gunther, more nervous than André, started to hit himself in the head.

"Stop it, you stupid ass! Do you hear me? Stop it before you mess her up."

Gunther stood quietly holding his head in both hands.

Snowflower walked across the stage as if she were floating on air, throwing kisses to the crowd, as André had suggested. Approaching the microphone once more, she started to croon a soft, musical tune.

"With all my heart I thank you,
even though I'm just a doll.
You've made my dreams come true.
I'll be your friend, whether you're big or small.
With all my heart, I love you all."

"Whew." André did flips across the stage as Snowflower slowly made her exit.

The crowd went crazy applauding.

André and Gunther led the small performer from the stage as the curtain closed. They quickly threw a large, enveloping cape around her, hurrying her into their dressing room where they made her "comfortable."

The dwarfs were ecstatic with the result of their first week of performance that included the space creature. They'd open a bottle of wine.

Snowflower and the mechanical man...... Frank was in the audience every day. Every night he'd practice before the mirror in his room.

The show at Digby-Hones was to run for two weeks, an unusually long gig for a promotion, but an exceptional one. In the middle of the second week's run, Frank decided to approach the managers, the dwarfs, about a job for himself with the group. He figured it was a crazy idea, but he felt compelled to ask.

The Mechanical Man

Facing André and Gunther, he stuttered out his request. "I...I wondered...that is...do you ever consider adding any help for the group...I mean..."

"For crap's sake, man, say what you mean!" André chomped on his soggy cigar butt.

"Well, I've been watching and practicing. I'd like to work for you...learn to be a mechanical man."

The dwarfs could hardly control their own excitement. "Are you any good?"

Frank's Adam's apple clunked up and down. "I don't know."

"Well, don't just stand there, let's see what you can do." André lit a new cigar.

Frank didn't move.

"Now!" André yelled.

Grabbing a cap from his back pocket, Frank started to emulate some of Leonard's best moves.

The clowns' eyes lit up with glee. This was better than they could have hoped for. The guy was good. Maybe better than good.

Being careful not to let Frank know what they really thought, André said, "Well, we might be able to use you fer a go-fer for a while 'til you learn. When could you start?"

"Right away!"

"Ain't you even interested in the bread?"

Frank looked puzzled.

"You know, the money? Well anyway, a hundred-fifty a week to start and yer keep. That's it."

"O.K.," Frank whispered.

"We'll move on in a little over a week."

Abby was stunned as her boy sat in the kitchen and tried to explain why he was joining a traveling road show. It made no sense to her, but it became very clear that he was adamant about it, and past experience had shown her that it was close to impossible to change her son's mind once he'd made it up.

Leonard hated Frank from the moment he first saw him. Think they're fooling ole Leonard with this helper stuff, he thought.

They think I'm going to teach this jerk the ropes. Like hell! Leonard refused to have anything to do with Frank. His drinking increased every day.

Making himself useful, Stein did whatever André told him to do, any job no matter how menial. For the first time in his life, he'd begun to feel as if he belonged somewhere.

Contacts with Snowflower were few and brief. He would pass the dwarfs with her going to and coming from the stage, or just hear André's voice, telling her gently, to come this way or go that way.

Saturday, December 10th, was the last show for the small troupe of performers at Digby-Hones. It dawned bright and cold.

Frank spent most of the day carrying and packing excess scenery and lights into the trailer they pulled behind the motorhome. André, biting and sputtering orders, his teeth clamped around the usual cigar stub, made sure Gunther had the rig lubricated, gassed up and ready for the road trip back to Ohio.

"We'll be off the tour for a month, Frank, for Christmas and rehearsals. I expect you to be ready to start replacing Leonard our first trip out in the new year."

Frank couldn't believe that he was going to get a chance to be the mechanical man. But if André said so, it had to be true.

Gunther, overly excited about heading back home, hurried to get Snowflower settled in their dressing room after the last show. He fixed her mobility circuits, leaving her there, but forgot to lock the dressing room door.

Leonard, stumbling and weaving, made his way through the empty hallway in the rear of the store toward the dwarf's dressing room. Two-fisting the door, he pounded, yelling, "Hey Mouth, do you hear me. Let me in or I'll huff and I'll puff an' I'll kick your door in!" Spittle drooled from the corner of his drunken mouth. Pushing harder on the door, he was surprised when it sprung open.

The room was dark as he staggered in. Trying to reach for a light switch, he tripped and fell on the floor. "Keeryst!" he bellowed. Looking up, he saw Snowflower sitting motionless in the gloom.

"There you are, dollbaby. Well, ain't you quiet now?" Snowflower's eyes glinted in the darkness.

"Cat got yer tongue?" He stood up menacingly close to the android. "They got you all drugged up or what?" With that, he fell against her legs grabbing her arms. "Talk, c'mon talk to me," he commanded.

"I am number 25. You must not interfere with my arms."

"Come to daddy, little girl. Let's have some fun."

Snowflower, with tremendous effort, attempted to raise her left arm. It was no use. She couldn't move. Leonard reached out and jerked hard on her arms. A shrill alarm sounded from her. It shrieked loud enough to almost shatter Leonard's eardrums. He dropped her back into the chair.

"Playin' tricks on ole Leonard are you? Well, we'll just see about that." He hit her full in the face with his fist.

Her head hit the wall with a thud.

The alarm shook the small room, as Snowflower's soft voice kept repeating, "...Do not interfere with my arms. I am number 25."

Leonard had just grabbed her again when Frank came crashing through the partially open door. He picked Leonard up and threw him through the open doorway. Higgin's head hit the metal door jamb. He lay there motionless, bleeding.

"Oh, Gawd! Oh, Gawd!" Frank ran to the immobile Snowflower.

"Are you all right? Did he hurt you?"

"I am not harmed. Can you help me?"

"Of course I'll help you. How?"

"Are you XC1?" The android waited for an answer.

Frank, deeply puzzled by her question and her inability to move, didn't answer except to ask her again if she was hurt. "Can you stand?"

"Not now. Carry me to the roof, I must send a signal. It is imperative; my energy source is running out. I cannot function much longer. If you are your true self, you will do as I ask."

Not understanding any of it, he lifted the doll creature into his arms. Sure on one hand that he was losing his mind, yet compelled by another force he could not name, he took her to the steps and carried her up to the roof. It was dark when he reached the old picnic table.

"Hold me upright on the table." He did as she told him. With his help, she raised her right arm, repeating the routine she had exhibited when she was first discovered on the hillside. The android kept turning in all four directions, her arm held up by Frank.

Baffled and becoming afraid, Frank stood beside her, waiting for the unknown.

Gunther was the one who found Leonard lying in a pool of his own blood. He knew the old man was dead before he ever touched him. Jumping up and down, and scurrying back and forth moaning, he didn't know what to do next.

André found him clomping down the dark hallway, squealing like a wounded pig. "They're gone and he's dead! Jesus, help us!"

"Who's gone and who's dead?" André jerked him to a stop grabbing him by the hair.

"Snowflower. Snowflower's gone. Leonard's lying in the hallway with his head bashed in...bloody. Blood's all over the place."

"Where's Frank?" André was getting impatient with his partner.

"They ain't around. He... he must be with her."

"How could she have gotten out of here, unless you didn't lock her up?"

Gunther, beating at his head again, started whimpering, "I forgot...I forgot...I forgot."

"I could kill you for this, you stupid moron!"

Racing through the hall with Gunther following, André led the way to the stairway to the roof. Climbing as fast as they could, they reached the metal, outside door. It wouldn't open. Pushing as hard as they were able, it refused to budge.

"Get down to the back exit. Get the fire axe off the wall."

André nearly pushed Gunther down the steps. He continued to work at the door.

Frank stood on the old, warped picnic table; he suddenly lost his equilibrium. A blinding flash of light pinpointed him and the android as they stood on the table.

"Hold my hand, XC1, and all will be well."

Doing what she told him to do, Frank knew he was no longer in control of anything. He felt himself being lifted, floating upward toward the light source. He was in a soporific state, not sure if he was asleep or awake. The force continued to lift him into a bruised, moonless sky. All the tension seemed to leave his body. When his head began to clear, he was standing in a small crystal-like room with Snowflower by his side. All four walls were of a heavy, clear crystal material, like glass. The walls appeared to be about three inches thick. The light that had seemed to carry them to this place was gone. The room was cool and comfortable.

"This is the Master Ship. We are safe here," Snowflower assured Frank.

A sudden hydraulic gasp signaled the opening of a large portal in one side of the small room.

"Come with me, XC1. I will take you to the others." Number 25 seemed to be rejuvenated. She led him down corridors, through sealed lock-rooms, over jig-saw puzzled, metal bridges, (and with alacrity), pulling a reluctant Frank behind her.

He was ill with fear and apprehension. The scar near his left eye was the deepest scarlet it had ever been, revealing his fright. What was she leading him into? Would the people (if they were people) help him, or was his life over.

Entering the huge control room, his eyes widened in amazement at the crew working silently over magnificently lit computer-like machines. He could see every color of the rainbow in the lights that brought the machines to life. Noise was infinitesimal.

Each worker on the bridge wore the exact same, flawlessly tailored jumpsuit. Each in various shades of green.

One by one, they turned to look at Frank. Each face an exact replica of his own! His legs buckled under him.

Snowflower braced him from behind. Her strong arms around his waist, she led him toward one of them saying, "Master, we have brought XC1 back to you as you commanded."

The Mechanical Man

Frank bolted, running back in the direction from which he had just come. The Master raised his hand, stopping him in mid-step without touching the young man in any way.

"You must not fear us for we are you and you are of us. We wish you only peace and happiness among us after your long, thirty-year sojourn on Earth. We are all one here. Your experimental time is over and another will take your place."

Frank stared straight ahead, his head ached, pounding like he had been hit by a hammer. His eyes watered. Fear clouded his vision. He wondered if it were all a dream.

It had taken the dwarfs ten minutes to force open the steel door to the roof. They had hacked and pushed in unison until they finally fell through the doorway like two rag dolls. Scurrying up onto their feet, they ran toward the picnic table. Frank Stein sat on the one bench by the table, mute, a surprised look on his face.

"Where is she? Kee-ryste. Stein, where is she?"

"They took her," was all he said.

Gunther started to jump up and down wailing, "I knew it! I knew it! We're too late."

"Shut up!" André clobbered Gunther over the head with his clenched fist. "We can't worry over her anymore. We gotta think about our biggest worry that's lyin' down there in the hallway. Stein, why in the hell did you have to kill him?"

Frank just shook his head.

"Both of you, c'mon, we'll have to hurry to clean up that mess before anyone sees it. Then we hafta get outta here tonight—quick."

Gunther and Frank meekly followed André down the stairs.

The three of them worked steadily for half an hour, cleaning up the bloody evidence, then stuffed Leonard's body into a wardrobe trunk which they placed in the scenery trailer. Frank worked listlessly, speaking only when spoken to.

"Hurry up." André was sweating so much that the drops of sweat were running down to the end of his ever-present cigar stub. "It's a good thing we don't have a show tonight. We'll have to sacrifice the bread. Just get yer asses into the RV and we'll get outta here fast."

Gunther continued his soft wailing as he got behind the wheel of the motor home. He headed north toward Route 75 with André screaming commands into his ear. Negotiating the entry ramp that had a severe curve in it was too much for the nervous Gunther. Failing the curve, he panicked, stepping on the brakes. The overloaded RV careened over the guard railing and fell 200 feet into a stony crevasse. It exploded into a horrendous fireball at the bottom. Both of the dwarfs were incinerated beyond recognition. Leonard's body was never accounted for. Frank Stein, although killed instantly, was thrown free of the fire and his body retrieved.

When Abby Stein reached the morgue to identify her son's body, Rabbi Berensen was standing by her side to comfort her.

After the funeral, Abby experienced gnawing perplexity about her son's death. She walked the bedroom floor at night rubbing her temples, gazing at Frank's high school graduation picture. She began to wonder if she was going to have a nervous breakdown.

The torment lingered.

"What was it? What was it?" She'd whisper to herself.

Two months after Frank's burial she remembered. The red, jagged scar that Frank had carried since he was ten years old. It had not been there on his face in death.

KEEP THE CHANGE

HE CALLED HIMSELF Amerigus Leonardo DeVictor. A short, dark man with a flowing black mustache and curly black hair framing a mostly bald head. DeVictor lived in a small clapboard house just off one of the main streets in town.

The little white house with the bright green roof was festooned with American flags. Across the back of the front porch, a long sign declared, "AMERIGUS LEONARDO DE VICTOR FOR MAYOR."

He had spent forty years of his sixty-five in the U.S.A. He had dug gravel from a large quarry for thirty-five years. When he retired, they gave him a gold watch.

People laughed behind his back, and some even laughed in his face. "Hey, Amerigus, you ready to run for President yet?" He was a neighborhood joke.

Leonardo let the insults roll off his back. He remained adamant in his resolve to be a good American and held to his dream to hold public office.

The only vice, if it can really be called a vice in this case, was his love for horses—race horses. He visited the track at least once a week, never betting on the races, but wandering around back and forth in the paddock area, watching, studying the horses one at a time, writing notes in a little notebook. He observed until he felt he knew each animal explicitly. Then he would pick the winners of each race, but only in his book. He became expert in his opinions. His dream was to own such a horse that would win the Kentucky Derby—another one of his fantasies.

Keep the Change

People around the track became used to seeing him. "Hi buddy! How's it going?" or "How do you like number six in the third?"

Amerigus smiled, waved, but said little. Then one afternoon he saw a sign announcing a local horse auction to be held in nearby Greenfield. It was an epiphany in the immigrant's life.

His old Plymouth chugged merrily along as Amerigus headed for the horse auction. The crowd in the big viewing barn was dense and noisy. One at a time the horses were brought into the arena to be led around. Then the auctioneer would start his chant, calling out bids, yelling, urging the crowd to bid higher.

A big black stallion danced at the end of its tether, nerves showing, hooves pounding into the dirt snorting his displeasure. He was beautiful, big, and obviously powerful.

Amerigus wrote a note beside the horses' name, FLASH GORDON...too independent, he wrote. Nevertheless, FLASH GORDON sold for $1,000,000 dollars.

Finally, near the end of the auction, a small chestnut gelding was led in. "Ladies and Gentlemen, this beautiful horse is KEEP THE CHANGE, sired by MAIN LINE and grandson of SLIDING IN, the great Derby winner."

There was little interest in the small horse with the long pedigree, except from Amerigus. He couldn't take his eyes off the shining chestnut horse.

Whispers ran through the crowd: "Likes to follow the field," or, "The horse won't run in front, only behind." And finally, the comment, "Too sociable."

Amerigus waited, listening to the low bids. Finally, the auctioneer was ready to strike his gavel on seventy-two thousand dollars when the little immigrant shouted, "Seventy-five thousand dollars!" The gavel fell and Amerigus Leonardo felt stunned—he'd bought himself a race horse!

The cashier who settled the pay-offs on the bids eyed the little man in the old black suit. "How do you want this handled?"

"Cash," Amerigus answered, as he dug deep into his inside coat pocket. Finally, his fist emerged clutching greenbacks.

"Man, you shouldn't be carrying that kind of money like that."

"Thank you for your concern, sir, but I had to come prepared."

He counted out seventy-five thousand dollars, signed all the papers, then with a perplexed look on his face he asked the cashier, "Where can I keep my horse?"

"Never owned a horse?"

"No, never!"

"Wait here for me until I'm through."

Amerigus liked his face, so he stayed put.

True to his word, the man returned. "C'mon, you'll have to buy a trailer for the horse first. There's lots of them for sale around the lot. By the way, I'm George Truman."

They settled on a bright, red trailer that had seen better days, but seemed structurally sturdy.

Amerigus was in a fog at this point. His brain twirling. What had he done? What had he done?

"I'm George Truman, Mr. DeVictor, and I know just the person for you to hook up with."

Hook up with? What was this hook up with?

But Amerigus had a trust for the man who was leading him around. They rigged up a temporary bumper hitch on the Plymouth and hooked on the horse trailer. George was telling Leonardo what to do when, finally, they were ready to depart the auction lot.

"Drive straight down this road to the first lane you see."

The old Plymouth was groaning under the load and Amerigus was sweating freely. "This the turn?" he asked.

"Yeah, turn in here and drive slow. It's a dirt road full of ruts."

Finally, after breathing dust for about a half mile, Truman yelled, "Stop!"

They were in front of an old, Victorian farm house that had forgotten what paint was.

"Mary, Mother of God, pray for us sinners." Amerigus crossed himself. "Now what?" he whispered.

"Just sit tight, I'll be right back." Truman walked up to the house.

A short, plump man with a ruddy face opened the door to George. They disappeared inside the house.

It wasn't long before a little girl with long red braids walked out onto the front porch. She waved at Amerigus, smiling a broad freckle-faced grin. Hopping down the steps she slowly approached the car.

"You got a horse in there?" She nodded toward the trailer.

Amerigus, unused to children, just gave her a little nod back.

"What kinda' horse is it?"

"A gelding." He figured that should stump her.

"How many hands?" the girl persisted.

"I'm not sure."

"Geez, I'll bet if I owned a horse I'd know how big he was. Can I see him? I love horses."

"I don't know. He might get nervous with more strangers."

"I promise, cross my heart, not to make him nervous."

Amerigus just couldn't resist the child. "Ooh, All right I'll let you see him."

Amerigus wanted to look him over again anyway. He crawled out of the car and opened the trailer just enough for them to look in.

"Gosh, Mister, you can't tell nothing from this end."

Amerigus had to agree.

About that time, the two men came up to the trailer. "Mr. DeVictor, I'd like you to meet Paddy Maquillan."

The two men shook hands. Amerigus liked Paddy's face, too.

"Paddy has agreed to take over the training of KEEP THE CHANGE, that is, if you are agreeable. He will provide a stall and keep for the horse, as well as the training."

Amerigus was overwhelmed. An answer to a dream.

"The pay will have to be discussed between you," Truman continued. "I hope you can afford this. Paddy's the best I know."

The little man rubbed his bald head and beamed. "Don't worry about money."

What they didn't know was that Amerigus Leonardo DeVictor was a millionaire. Amerigus had scrimped and saved and invested wisely for forty years.

Paddy put his arm around the little girl. "This is my granddaughter, Molly, who's always underfoot." He laughed and pulled on one of her braids. "Her grandmother and I have raised her from a baby. She's ten years old."

They took KEEP THE CHANGE out of the trailer, leading him to his new home in the horse barn behind the house. It was clean and well-kept for an old stable. The stall for the little gelding was roomy and sweet smelling. Molly danced around the horse in utter delight, while Amerigus kept touching its velvety nose and whispering sweet Italian words in the horse's ear. The horse was destined to be loved a lot... it was obvious.

Soon, the stall was decorated with American flags by the proud owner of the little horse. Of course, it was decided his silks would be red, white, and blue. Paddy started training the two-year-old immediately. Not small enough himself to ride the horse on its 5:30 a.m. laps around the track, he found a local apprentice jockey, Alvaraz, to take on the job.

The training of KEEP THE CHANGE went on for months, and seemed unending to Amerigus, who visited his horse at least three times a week, petting and whispering to his gelding.

Finally, Paddy said he was ready for his first race. A local run at the nearby track.

Race day saw Amerigus pacing back and forth in front of the paddock while Molly followed Paddy until he was nearly distracted with her. "Shoo. Go out and keep Mr. DeVictor company."

The trumpet sounded the race to begin. Leonardo nearly fainted. He was very nervous as KEEP THE CHANGE proudly strolled toward the starting gate. His patriotic silks seemed to sparkle on the young, apprentice jockey's youthful body.

The bell rang, the gate opened, and the horses broke.

It was a field of eight. The track was perfect, just slightly damp. KEEP THE CHANGE broke good in fifth position near the inside rail. His pace steady and focused... focused, that is, on the rear ends of the first four horses. He seemed content to hold that place as the other horses vied for better positions.

After the last turn before the finish, he was still fifth even though Alvarez, his jockey, was pounding him pretty hard with his crop.

Amerigus hung his head while Molly cried. Paddy, never down, said, "Just remember, that's his first race for us. We can't expect too much yet. We have a long way to go, but we'll get there."

In the paddock, KEEP THE CHANGE nibbled hay in his stall and rubbed his itchy back against the wall that was covered with the American flag. He was content.

The next race was at the county fair and was just a repeat performance of the first.

Paddy finally announced to the little band of fans that the gelding was entered in the Alahambra Stakes, and come hell or hot fire, he'd cure him of following his friends.

The Alahambra Stakes was a festive occasion with much hoop-dee-do and a lot of betting. Needless to say, KEEP THE CHANGE was last on the parimutuel board.

Although it was against Amerigus' belief to gamble, he thought that he should show some support for his little chestnut gelding, so he put one hundred dollars on him to win. He felt guilty throwing the money away.

Molly rubbed CHANGE down, and kissed his velvety nose before he left the paddock. Paddy led him proudly from the stall.

Alvaraz saddled him and mounted the little horse.

As usual, KEEP THE CHANGE (number 6) was easy to get into the gate. The bell rang, the horses broke fast on a sloppy, wet track. FLASH GORDON, the million dollar horse, Leonardo had pegged as "too independent," strained to be a front runner, almost bumping one horse into the inside rail. He slipped and threw his rider down hard. Fortunately, the jockey was thrown over the railing onto the grass with no injuries.

CHANGE rolled his eyes in surprise and shadowed the number three horse. The five leaders were bunched up pretty close as they rounded the home turn and there, sitting on the outside rail, was Molly frantically waving a rather large American flag and urging KEEP THE CHANGE to "Run! Go! Go! Go! Go!" she kept screaming.

When that horse saw her with that flag, it must have meant going home to him, and that damned horse took off like a NASA rocket. He blew them all away. Number 6 flashed on the board to the amazement of hundreds of people.

In the winner's circle, Amerigus Leonardo DeVictor stood beside his horse with tears in his eyes.

Molly, by his side, was just speechless for the first time in her young life.

Paddy walked up to the proud owner and shook his hand.

"Now," Amerigus whispered in the gelding's ear, "Now we go for the Kentucky Derby." The horse nodded his head up and down.

Then, Amerigus remembered he had to collect on his bet.

THE RETURN

I SIT IN the rusting old wreck of a car, daring a growling mutt to spring at me. The car is doorless, no wheels either; it's set up on cement blocks like a nightmare sculpture. A piece of junk that was once my get-around car.

What great sage was it that said you can't go home? Well, he was wrong. Here I am, back in my old "haunts," as my grandmother would have said. My old haunts—gawd! It must be a haunting for me to show myself here again after what I done. It was a long journey to get here, though.

I look out over the pasture, left fallow, then toward the barn, paint peeling off the boards. The barn door standing open, turning a blind, dark eye my way, accusing. The old dilapidated farmhouse, shutters askew, standing ghostly empty. The windows, partially boarded up, making me think of a battered fighter, only all the fight is gone from this place.

The lane looks unused, but I'll soon be walking up to the house to look in.

Screeching brakes break the silence. A red pickup bounces along the curve in the country road. Teenagers are aboard, screaming their delight. The mutt takes off in their direction. That is good, 'cause I don't want to cut the dog up. I feel around my belt for my hunting knife. It must be there. It ain't. I musta dropped it somewhere. Feel naked without my knife.

I see the sheriff's car turn into the lane. It's better if I hide. Sliding behind the front seat of the

The Return

old car, I watch Sheriff Blaney drive right by me and park the car in front of the house. Don't think he'd be happy to see me back. He worked real hard to make sure I'd be sent away for good. His florid face is still set in a determined scowl. Never was a very pleasant guy. He pulls a sign from the trunk of his car. Carefully picking his way up the rotting steps, he proceeds to nail a red sign with black letters next to the front door. Can't see what it says from where I am, but I'll get close enough to read it soon.

Old Blaney drives away with a roar. Can't help laughing 'cause he missed seeing me.

If I was smart, I'd probably leave this place, but hell, I haven't even looked into the house yet. A sadness hits me when I look at the bad shape the farm is in. Knowing that I caused most of the trouble around the place—the family gone, an' all. That is, the family that was left after... Damn! I really flew off, didn't I?

Guess I'll just go up an' look in the house. The sign says, "THIS PROPERTY CONDEMNED." C'mon, I tell myself, pull a board off the window. Cupping my hands up to the window, I peer through the dirty glass. It looks funny in there... strange. The old sofa still sags in the middle, an' stuffing leaks through what was once green upholstery. Used to like to sit there with Amelia, my wife, in the evenings watching television after supper. The family usually gathered around. Mom, Dad, Jake, my brother...

Beautiful Amelia, lovely Amelia, liar Amelia, faithless Amelia. The television's gone with nearly everything else. It's a real dump now. Strange, once I thought of it as a warm sanctuary, a place I belonged. No more.

Something moved. I could see it out of the corner of my eye. I turned just in time to see a woman disappear into the black hole doorway to the barn. Amelia, it musta been Amelia. But then, I guess that couldn't be.

Suddenly, I don't like being back. Can't go near the darkness in the barn. Don't have my knife. The wind blows through my short, dark hair. A chill seems to enter my bones. It's getting darker, almost night. I feel like an old man. Hell, I'm only thirty-nine. A storm roils in the ill-omened clouds, lightning cuts through the sky, dancing its warnings.

My feet carry me against my will toward the barn. I strain to open the old wooden door wider. So dark. In the silence, a laugh. A man and a woman are laughing. Close my ears, I tell myself—don't want to see them again, but my eyes search out the two. There in the darkness of the barn are my brother Jake, and my wife, Amelia, embracing... kissing. He's touching her breast. She smiles up at him starting to unbutton her blouse.

Everything goes red. My knife is in my hand. It flies in the darkness like lightning, ripping, slashing, cutting, stabbing, and then it's over. I stand there covered with blood, my overalls wet with it, my head bursting. My father standing behind me, then he's running away. I'm alone then with the devastation I've inflicted.

But, that was a long time ago. There have been different cells in different jails that have held me since the trial. My remorse is overwhelmed by my memories of the betrayal by my own brother and my wife. When finally, ten years after my conviction, all of my appeals were gone, the sentence of death held firm.

How I got here is a mystery to me. Didn't I feel the needle of death? Memory fails me. I only know that being here is hellish. I must leave.

Walking down the lane, I see purple violets are growing. Amelia loved them so. The old car is there waiting—I go and sit behind the broken steering wheel, then I know that tomorrow will be the same as today. I will endure the betrayal and the killing again. So it will be every day. I know now that this is hell.

MAUSOLEUM

IT SEEMED only right, to Marta, that David Slater should offer her the starring role in his latest blockbuster, thriller, MAUSOLEUM. The offers for her services were definitely waning. If anyone could turn that around, it was David!

There was little doubt about it, time was making headway on Marta's face. She was looking into her floor length mirror in her lavishly furnished, pink bedroom, "Gawd! Janna, just look at the tiny lines around my eyes!"

Janna Veraux, her trainer, refused to be sucked into any part of that conversation.

"Maybe a little age gives my face more character?"

The question was not answered, as Janna continued to pack up her workout bag.

Shunning a facelift, Marta told herself that she could carry it off like Bacall, as a natural beauty.

At forty, Marta Krista had been a movie star longer than she cared to recall. It had taken her what seemed like a lifetime to rise to the pinnacle of a David Slater picture, but it hadn't taken her nearly that long to share her bed with him. They'd come up the ladder in Hollywood together. She worked on one small project after another, getting little chance to do any real acting. She found herself being used mainly as beautiful window dressing in sexy, for male, nominated action films. Slowly, Marta's tenacity paid off when she was named one of the ten most sought after leading ladies in "movieville."

David met her in the early days while he, too, struggled for recognition as an up-and-coming director who was striving to be taken seriously. Marta had taken him home and to her bed before he was SLATER. Her influence helped raise him from a lowly assistant director to what he is today, a film titan. They never married. Somehow, David never got around to asking her and she didn't push. They were referred to as the "magic couple", and the columnists called them "...that gifted director and his raven-haired beauty." Slater was a tall, board of a man with greying blonde hair and a large boney face, his cheekbones set high. Not handsome, but he drew women.

Marta, completing her workout on the exercycle, stopped it abruptly calling out, "Don't bother with anything else today, Janna. I'll set the whirlpool. Just take off; I won't need you anymore today."

The trainer nodded, picked up her practice bag, waved goodbye and left.

Walking toward the full length mirror, Marta pulled off her sweatshirt then stopped to take off her brief, exercise suit. She stood in front of the mirror, squinting her eyes, inspecting her naked body, running her small, white hands down her bare hips. No cellulite, she thought to herself... still silky and slim. Her breasts, always her best feature, were round and firm. As she pushed them up, cupping one in each hand, the nipples became erect. "Not bad there either!" she commented out loud. Turning to look at her backside, she laughed a little, remembering David saying she had the best ass in town!

She pushed her stormy-black hair back from her face. Her eyes were black and incandescent as she smiled at her reflection. "Oh, hell! What are a few tiny lines?" she asked herself aloud.

Anxious to get back to work, she had been pressing David about a start date for the film. He seemed to put her off. It puzzled her. Other things were bothering her, too. He hadn't been coming home in the evenings as early as usual, often arriving after she went to bed. The sun-washed Malibu beach house had always been a refuge for him. When he did show up, his mind seemed to be somewhere else. Their lovemaking had slowed to a once-in-a-while occurrence. Silly rumors were being circulated, by the dirty gossip rags, that David Slater had a new "main squeeze" hidden away in some house, in some canyon. Marta told herself that they were all lies. She wished David would sue the tabloids.

The call to report for work finally came. She could quit torturing herself with doubts and settle down to the business of making a film. The movie would be a comeback for her, of sorts. She hadn't made a picture for two years. This could establish her again as the fine actress she knew she was.

Closing herself in her bedroom at 7 p.m., she didn't hear Slater arrive home early that evening. He worked quietly at his desk in the oceanfront study. At ten o'clock, the telephone rang shrilly, breaking the silence. Marta, upstairs in her bedroom, awakened, startled by the sudden jangling. She had forgotten to disconnect her phone. Annoyed, she turned toward the offending instrument, wondering who had answered it. Carefully, she lifted the receiver to her ear.

"Slater? J. L. here."

"Sure J. L. How's everything?"

"Things aren't so good on my end."

J. L. Levin was David's executive producer.

"What's wrong? Can I help?"

Always the helper, Marta thought as she listened. She hated the habit he had of being on everyone's side at the same time.

"It's the big boys at Bay Industries; they aren't happy with your choice of a leading lady. I told you not to hire her for the part!"

"Well, hell, J. L., she's always been a big draw. This is a helluva time to tell me this!"

"The money boys think her drawing days are over."

"Gawd damn, J. L., what do you expect me to do at this late date?"

"I expect you to be smart and fire her!"

"That's not going to be an easy thing to do."

"Look, Slater, everyone else knows she's washed up...too old for the part. Bayside said if you keep her, they're going to pull out."

"They can't do that! We have a contract."

"Better not try them."

"Listen, give me a few days to figure out the best thing to do. All right?"

"Three days, that's it. Tell the press she's sick...or she's broken both legs..., anything, but get rid of her! Understand?"

"I'm trying to understand. Goodnight."

The director heard no answer from the other end of the line, just a loud click.

Marta bit her lip, drawing blood, hoping she wouldn't scream as she silently replaced the telephone receiver onto its cradle.

A few minutes later David entered her bedroom and crawled into bed beside her. He was particularly tender. She endured his lovemaking, hating him every minute. Hadn't she made him what he was today, she reasoned... Marta Krista's director that she'd brought along the whole, clawing way.

She lay there in the darkness, her mind racing in fast forward as she pictured Slater sitting across from her in her dressing room making up lies to tell her why she would be replaced in the film. Then, her mind wandered back as she remembered the incident, about a week ago, when she was driving to a hair appointment. She saw David entering one of the small, exclusive jewelry stores that dot Rodeo Boulevard in Beverly Hills.

Slowly, she pulled her small sports car around the corner from the store and parked it. Walking casually toward the jewelry store show window, she saw David in earnest conversation with a salesman. The two men were leaning over a tray of what looked like loose diamonds. She turned quickly, tears covering her cheeks, and ran toward her car.

Driving away, she asked herself, diamonds for whom? For *her,* of course! The one in the canyon house... The one, she now believed he had been romancing for months. Didn't the gossip rags say so?

The next morning on the set Marta stood in the darkness of the huge faux-mausoleum. She stood there in the place for a long time. Her blood-red fingernails were digging into the palms of her hands. She was, once again, biting her lower lip and her chin quivered. Her long black hair shined around her perfectly made-up face. The red dress she wore was torn at the shoulder and slit to the hip. The costume designer's idea of the perfect dress for a death scene.

She listened from the depths of the mausoleum watching as David Slater called out his commands and walked off the distance in front of the set. At fifty, he remained ruggedly sexy.

"Remember, Joe, the light must be full on Marta's face when she emerges out of the darkness."

"Full on her face!" Joe, the lighting director, repeated to his assistant. "Apparently he hasn't looked closely at her face recently. She's got more wrinkles than a well-used road map!" His voice seemed to be caught like an echo in the massive set.

Marta stepped deeper into the shadows of the cavernous fake building. Tears were streaking her make-up. David would be calling her soon expecting her to slide into the camera's view like a svelte cat. Then he'd come to her trailer and tell her the lies.

Words were echoing in her head..."washed up...too old for the part..." all the words she'd heard on the telephone the night before.

David called her name. Marta did not appear. "Damn that woman!" he cursed to himself. When she failed to appear after the second call, he walked back into the inky, black interior of the set with a flashlight in his hand, looking for her. Deeper and deeper into the mausoleum he walked, softly calling her name. He was startled when he bumped into her nearly knocking her down. She was leaning against a wooden supporting beam. She stood there trance-like, staring into nothing.

"Marta, what in the name of God is wrong with you?" He shook her slightly by the shoulders.

"Do you love me, David?" Her arms went around his waist, her ear against his heart.

"Good God! Marta, this isn't the time or place for that now."

"Do you love me, David?" She whispered it against his chest.

Deciding to humor her, "Have you ever doubted it?"

The small black gun was carefully hidden in the folds of her dress. He did not see it appear in the darkness. Pushing it against his side she pulled the trigger three times. As he fell at her feet, a small, blue, velvet box slid out of his shirt pocket. Marta never saw it. Another shot rang out in the darkness echoing through the now lifeless set.

Joe got there first. They were lying together.

The lighting director knelt over them to feel for a pulse. They were both dead. The blood-soaked velvet box lay nearby. When it hit the floor, the lid had sprung open revealing a huge pear-shaped diamond ring.

Joe knelt there shaking his head. Looking up at his assistant, he said, "Can you figure this? Slater told me this morning that he was going to risk his future on this picture and keep Marta on. Not only that, he was planning on asking her tonight to marry him. He really loved the old broad!

THE FINGER OF GOD

IRA GASPED, as he always did, when the elevator whisked him upward, upward, upward, as if heading for the heavens. It always took his breath away and he tugged out a wrinkled handkerchief from his rear pants pocket. Adjusting his grey serge pants, he then mopped his bald shining head flicking at the fringe of grey hair around his ears. He'd been coming to the "top of the world" for two years, almost every month since he arrived from Russia. It seemed to him that in some way it repaid his debt to God. It seemed as if the building itself might be the finger of God sticking up over New York for all of his little immigrants to visit so they could behold the miracle He had wrought for them.

It amused Ira to consider the new Empire State Building the finger of God. But whatever he called it, for certain, it was a miracle.

He walked from the bank of elevators out onto the observation platform preparing himself for the awe that always came to him while looking at New York City from up there. It was 1933 and, even if the streets weren't lined with gold, it was a wondrous place to him.

Humming a little tune, he slowly moved around the observation platform. He saw her from the corner of his eye. She was leaning on the concrete railing peering down. A young woman looking sweetly naive in her calf-length, blue pleated dress and penciled Garbo eyebrows, her hair bent into deep dents by a marcel iron. Up to date in every way, and so sadly beautiful that it made Ira's heart hurt a little.

He moved closer to her and his nostrils were filled with the light scent of gardenia perfume. She didn't notice him. She just kept staring, in a compelling way, into a crevasse that held the spikes of other lesser, man-made hives still misted over in the mid-morning light.

The little man in the lumpy suit and the blonde girl were alone at one corner of the viewing place. His gut feeling kept him from moving on.

She means to jump or at least she seems to be considering it, he thought.

"Oh God! Please help me to say the right thing here."

Like a tour guide, the little Jewish tailor started to talk. "This building has one hundred and ten floors above the ground," he said, "and is serviced by sixty-seven elevators. It is the tallest building in the world! Think of that, in the whole *world!*"

The girl lifted her tear-streaked face and looked at Ira as if he were crazy.

He went on, moving closer to her, "And yes, on a clear day, you can see for fifty miles." He pointed his finger out toward the city and gently touched her elbow, his fingers urging her to lean back toward him as he continued to talk. "It took 60,000 tons of steel to build it and contains 2,153,000 square feet of rental space."

She moved toward him, allowing him to walk her slowly toward the exit doors and the elevators. He touched her hand, then forced himself to laugh, "Oh the building has had its downside, too; it's known as the most famous jumping off place in the city. Poor souls should be reminded that such an act is only a permanent solution to a temporary problem, and not solved like that."

The girl wept as Ira very gently held on to her arm, guiding her into a going down elevator. They were swiftly lowered toward Fifth Avenue.

Epilogue

The Empire State building has not been the tallest building in the world for many years.

A high fence was later built to stop jumpers.

HUSH

THE FIRST TIME I saw her was in a nightclub where the smoke machine hardly worked and the blues wailed through the smoke calling to the crowd like a pied piper. It was a small joint in old Hollywood where mostly forgotten horn players showed up to blow off memories and dope. But there was a good old trumpet man that weekend. The dump was crowded.

Looking across the noisy room, I saw her sitting with a group of young people, obviously already reaching a reeling high. Hell, I thought to myself, she's a baby. Couldn't be more than sixteen. That wrenched my gut a lot because she was so gawddamn gorgeous. What brought kids like her into places like this; what were they looking for?

I was there for a story...any story that would embarrass, titillate, startle or surprise the readers of the rag I worked for. I watched for celebs and their dirty laundry.

Something happened to me as I gazed across the small dance floor that night. I couldn't keep myself from looking at her red hair, pink lips, and fantastic body, which was covered by a black net halter top and mini skirt showing off her slender hips. I hadn't gotten a look at her eyes yet, but I would before my cameraman and I left.

Across the room, on the other side, sat my story...Tony Strata, movie star, womanizer, single, and at forty, still looking for a good lay when the feeling moved him. He was with a sexy-looking blond. A huntress whose blue eyes wandered constantly. I'd seen her before with various male actors. She'd paid her dues and tonight I'd get her name. She'd make the paper next week. That's what she hit the sheets for...publicity and hope.

I flat-footed my way across the dance floor while the band took a break. Someone recognized me, calling out something about my ancestry. Most of the younger ones knew me as "Hush-Hush," the name of the rag-mag I worked for. Cal Magee, my cameraman and investigator, followed closely on my heels. Sometimes I had to remind myself that my real name was Jackson Lee...free, white and forty-one years of age. I was assistant editor of a 'zine that existed on innuendo, even though some readers and subjects called them lies.

Cal moved around Strata's table snapping pictures while I pulled in an extra chair to join the group. "Who asked you to join the party?" Strata was quarrelsome and a little drunk.

"Now, Tony, surely you don't mind sharing a few minutes of your time with a friend."

"Like what friend? Certainly not you."

I could see he wasn't going to be very cooperative.

"No need to be upset with me and Cal. We're just doing our jobs. How about introducing me to the young lady?"

"Beat it." Strata yelled at us as he emptied his glass and pointed to the bartender for another.

"C'mon, Tony. We just want to give her a mention in next week's edition."

The girl started to push at her hair, then straightened her brief top. She snuggled up to Tony, her eyes on his face, "It won't hurt anything, honey, just a picture of us. I'd like it."

"For Christ's sake, can't anyone leave me alone for a minute?" He pushed her away. "All right, all right...give the snoop your name; then you take one picture of us together." He nodded at Cal. "Then both of you get lost or there'll be trouble."

Mission accomplished for me, Cal, and Miss Jewel Fancy.

"Gawd, how'd she think that name up?" Cal mumbled to me.

Walking back across the floor to the table we were occupying, I managed to weave my steps close to the gorgeous kid's group.

She was looking up just as I passed by and her eyes were two green emeralds.

Time has a way of passing when you're having fun, but hell, I wasn't having much fun. It must have been a month after the Strata picture was in the mag that I decided to venture up Hollywood Boulevard again. I told myself I was looking for a story, but I'd left Cal out of this expedition because I was really itching for another look at that gorgeous kid. Why?

I don't know. A short, fat, half-bald writer wasn't gonna do any scoring with her. And, hell, I didn't even know her name, not to mention she was jail bait for me.

When I got to the club it was closed, for good, that is until some other sucker opens it again, I thought. My feet led me half a block down the street to another dump that seemed to be rockin'. With nothing else planned, I nosed in. It took me a minute or two to get my eyes accustomed to the dark and another few minutes for my ears to tolerate the stuff the band was blasting out on oversized speakers. The sound hit me in the chest like a heart attack.

Peering through the crowd, I spotted her in the back. She was with the same gang as before, only this time they seemed lifeless. Shoving through the dancers, I headed for the bar.

Ordering a bottle of beer (no glass please), I settled onto a fake leather and chromium stool that tilted a bit crazily.

I could see the doll clearly from there. No one seemed to notice me.

Out on the dance floor, they started to dance—if you can call it that—never touching each other and about two feet apart while the guy watched her tits jiggle.

Careful to ease my way toward her, I stepped in front of the boyfriend as I tried to move like what they called dancing.

"Hi!" I smiled down at her and kept trying to shuffle my feet. She looked at me like I was a piece of spoiled meat. "I don't talk to strangers." She turned her back away from me. About that time the place was invaded by a bunch of cops and the clientele went nuts trying to get out of the joint before anyone got busted.

Pulling her by her wrist, I jerked her into the men's room which was empty, "C'mon, hurry, hurry."

I continued to pull her arm. A window was open in the rear of the crapper. I pushed her through with me following fast.

She seemed to understand what was happening and cooperated.

Once we hit the dark alley it was only a few yards to my old, gray Mercedes parked up against the back of the building. I opened the passenger door and she jumped in without any encouragement. I hopped into the driver's seat, kicked the engine into a roar, and we shot out of that alley leaving a trail of blue smoke behind.

She screamed and I thought she was scared.

Uh-uh. It was followed by another sound—laughing like I never heard. She was loving it, the faster the better.

After about five minutes of driving I asked her, "Where do you want to go?"

She was leaning out the open window on the passenger side, her red hair flowing in the wind, an excited look in her green eyes. "To the moon!" she shouted. "To Miami South Shore."

Her small hands were over her ears as if she was closing out the world.

I drove her to my place in the Hollywood hills.

When we landed in my driveway, she started to show signs of disappointment. "Who lives here?"

"I do."

"You got anything in there?" Her meaning was clear to me.

"Naw, all out. Besides I'm not a user."

"Too bad. Don't know what you're missing." She was obviously coming down. "I'm kind of hungry." She yawned, stretching those incredibly shapely arms.

I wished they were around my neck.

My house had always seemed plenty big enough for me, but that night it felt small, cramped, and messy. I started picking up clothes and papers. The girl pitched her own claim out on the white sectional couch that took up most of the room.

It was the first time I realized it was no longer white, but a sort of grimy gray. She was asleep before I could hang up my coat.

The refrigerator, unlike the house, was well stocked.

I liked to cook. A half hour later, I had an omelet, bacon, toast, and coffee ready for my special guest and myself.

"Hey, wake up! Soup's on."

She opened those emerald eyes and stared at me. "Who are you?"

"Your guardian angel... maybe. C'mon, let's eat."

She stirred, kicked off her small golden sandals, and hopped up onto her feet. I guided her to the kitchen table.

The meal, though not gourmet, was well received. She ate heartily and drank two cups of coffee.

"Thanks Mr. Hush, it was good. Now, I gotta go home."

"You're welcome, sugar. By the way what is your name?"

"Georgia Maine."

"No, for real, what's your real name?"

"That's it, Georgia Maine. My mother had a sense of humor and I don't stay nights."

"O.K. Georgia, let's go. I'll take you. Where's home?"

"Pasadena...I live in Pasadena. Just drive and I'll point the way."

She slept during the whole trip from my place in North Hollywood to the correct Pasadena turn off.

"Colorado Boulevard. I'll show you the way," she said.

I followed her directions through a grid of dark streets I didn't know existed. Finally, she pointed me toward a ramshackle old carriage house in front of an old mansion.

"This is it." She hopped out of the car running toward the stairs leading to the second floor. She waved as she went through a door.

I sat there like a cigar store Indian who had just been knocked on his ass. I don't remember driving home.

I heard about the search for a teen-aged sex kitten needed to fill a role in Jack Chamber's new blockbuster, *The Miracle Tree*. In fact, Hush-Hush was running a contest to help find a new face for the picture.

Georgia Maine's face danced before my eyes, but where the hell was she? I'd tried four or five times to locate her, but no such name in the Pasadena phone book and she didn't show up at the joints with the kids.

The first week of the contest there were one hundred young wannabes champing at the bit to be tested for the part. They all paled in comparison to Georgia Maine...if that was her name.

Then, something pulled me back to Hollywood Boulevard and some of the dumps that appealed to the teen-aged set. The first two places full of young drinkers and druggies there was no sign of Georgia. In the third one I struck gold, or pyrite—she was there.

After a careful approach, I stood beside her at the crowded table. "Hi Georgia." Her head turned taking me in.

"Well, Mr. Hush, what brings you here?" Her little girl voice sounded like music to me.

"We have to talk."

"Why?" She was going to be stubborn.

"Now listen, damn it. In my pocket, I have a chance for you to become a star."

"A star what?"

"A movie star."

"I don't want to be a movie star."

The crowd was leaving the table. "Don't be foolish. This is the chance of a lifetime."

She rolled the emeralds at me, then surprised me with a good question. "What's all this have to do with you?"

"Oh, I see, you think this is a come on—well it isn't, babe. Just listen to me for five minutes."

I guess she figured she was safe enough with me there for five minutes, so she listened.

January's Hush-Hush had all the inside dope (or should I say info?) about the new starlet headed for the ingénue lead in Chamber's big movie, *The Miracle Tree*. Georgia Maine smoldered on the silver screen, just like I knew she would.

The unfortunate part of this story is that Tony Strata was cast as the romantic lead in "Tree." If Georgia was never impressed by anything else in Hollywood, she was impressed with Tony Strata. The man placed a hypnotic spell over the seventeen-year-old. (She'd had a birthday since I met her.)

Strata, old enough to be her father, sparkled like a teenager around the kid. If you'll excuse the expression, he really sucked her in.

Georgia started worrying about whether or not her hair suited Strata, or her clothes suited Strata, or if her make-up pleased Strata. Strata, Strata, Strata. She lived for him alone. My heart sank telling me there was big trouble ahead.

If there was anything Tony Strata could not tolerate, it was dope. It seems his own father had been a junkie and a couple of scars on the star's back were left there by an extension cord wielded by his stoned old man. He knew what dope could do.

Texas was hot and dusty the summer they shot *Miracle Tree*. But, if Texas was hot, so was the affair between Strata and Georgia Maine. They tried to keep it quiet; after all she was still jailbait. Insiders on the set were very aware of what was going on and made sure Georgia was on the arm of the latest young hunk at all special occasions.

Sooner or later, they would both disappear from the festivities leaving their dates to their own devices. It was an open secret. Tony looked good—well exercised, tanned to perfection.

Georgia, too, looked wonderful. Skin smooth and the color of a porcelain doll.

I took her to lunch one day to interview her about her life in Hollywood.

Unlike her former ideas about the place, she now painted it as ideal.

I wondered.

When we left the restaurant, the paparazzi almost knocked her over.

The cameras snapped at every angle possible. I even jumped one joker lying on the ground trying to shoot up her skirt. I punched him in the chops. It was chaos.

The *Miracle Tree* wrapped the end of June. I didn't see or hear much about Georgia after that.

Of course, there was the usual publicity about the movie and the stars were interviewed on all the talk shows.

I did get to see her on the *TODAY* show one morning. She looked ravishing and young.

Rumors were spreading that she and Strata were going to marry. Neither one would confirm or deny.

Variety had a brief headline: "Strata to do remake of Harvey."

The film was to be shot in Vancouver for some reason...probably money.

It was shortly after I read that, I ran into Georgia at a studio press luncheon. She was with four or five hangers-on. They were making a lot of noise.

When she saw me come in, she followed me and Cal to a table.

I told Cal to get lost.

"How are things going?" I spoke first.

"They're going just crappy, if you want to hear the truth."

Picking up my napkin and tossing it across my lap, "I want to hear the truth."

"Life stinks!" She sat down.

"What about the boyfriend?"

"He's just finished filming *Harvey*. I'm still busy doing publicity for *Tree*. I hate it." She pouted beautifully.

Just then Strata walked in with a young, well-endowed red head wearing a sun dress. They seemed to be more than just acquaintances. His hands carelessly caressed her bare shoulders as he stepped behind her to whisper in her ear. If he meant to put on a show with the girl, he succeeded.

Georgia ran from the area before I even had a chance to stop her. It was a crushing blow to a kid who wasn't used to Hollywood games...especially Tony Strata's games.

That night, as I remember it, seems like the culmination of a dream sequence in a bad B movie.

I was working at my desk late when my phone rang. It was my photographer, Cal.

"Your girlfriend's fallen over the edge," he said. "Way over the edge. Got stoned in some joint on the strip."

"Are you there now?" I was almost afraid to ask. "Can you keep an eye on her 'til I get there?"

"Yeah, and yeah. I'll do my best."

"I'm on my way."

It was a good three miles from my office to Vine Street. I pushed the accelerator in the old Mercedes hard to the floor.

My cell phone rang. "Yeah!"

"This is me, Cal. She's taking off in her car. Looks like she's heading for the canyons. I'll stay with her and you can follow as soon as you can."

There was only one reason she'd head up through the canyons, and that was Tony Strata.

I drove along waiting for Cal's directions. They never came. He didn't call again, leaving me to fumble around trying to find Strata's house. It took me an hour and a half before I found the place. I let the car drift into the steep driveway and shut off the motor. Lights were on all over the house.

Cal's VW was parked near the front entrance. The front door was open.

I stepped into the vestibule nearly falling over a man's body. It was Cal.

Then I saw Tony Strata through the entrance to the living room. He was sitting upright on the white carpeting, leaning against the huge stone fireplace. On his face, there was the look of total surprise. Part of his iconic face was gone.

As I leaned over Cal once more to feel for a pulse, I felt cold steel against my temple.

Clenching my teeth so hard, I felt my new bridge crack. As I turned my head; cold green eyes were looking into mine. It was hard for me to remember how those eyes smoldered on the silver screen.

Through the phlegm that was filling my throat, I managed to whisper, "I can help you, Georgia, if you'll let me." Was I pleading or asking a question? I guess both.

The Glock 9mm she held looked like a cannon in her small, well-manicured hand. She was pointing it right between my eyes. After I spoke, it wavered away from my allergic sinuses a little.

"Lie down on the floor beside your fat, hired garbage collector, he won't mind."

I hesitated.

"Now. On the floor," she repeated.

It was clear that Cal Magee was dead as hell and that I might follow him.

Georgia looked like anyone but the highly-publicized sex kitten whose face and form seemed to be on dozens of mag covers. Her red hair was hanging in strings that were not combed or sprayed at a Rodeo Drive salon. Her mascara was running black rivers down her pale cheeks, and the trademark lips, so plump and over extended, were quivering. She was barely wearing a black halter-topped silk dress.

As I lay on the luxurious carpet next to Cal, I felt something sticky and cold on my arm. Cal's blood! I inched away from his body.

I was sweating heavily. "I can help you, Georgia, if you'll tell me how this all happened and why. I'll get you out of here, if you want me to." Funny thing was, I meant it.

The gun was once again dancing in front of my eyes. The hand holding it shaking too much. It occurred to me that she might pull the trigger by accident.

She pushed her face closer to mine. "You help me? All you've ever done is to ruin my life every chance you could. Hush-hush, Mr. Lee, I'm writing the headlines now."

"Why don't we talk? Put the gun down and let's reason this out. There's got to be a way out of this for you."

"What you mean is, a way out of this for you, Mr. Headlines." She started to laugh, that silly little giggle the world would hear in all the sex scenes she'd done with Tony.

It must not have been acting, then. It was real, that laugh. I should care about those things now. "C'mon, let's talk, Georgia."

She sat down beside me, the gun still clenched in her fist. "I really loved him, you know."

"Really loved who?"

Keep her talking, I said to myself.

"Tony. He was all I cared about." She moaned to herself rocking her body a little, that million-dollar body. "He told me he'd marry me, if I stayed clean for three months while he was on location.

"May I sit?"

She didn't seem to hear me.

I sat up very carefully. "Go on, Georgia, I'm listening. Did you?"

"Did I what?"

"Did you stay clean?"

She rocked herself some more and wailed low in her throat like an injured dog. "I stayed clean," she sobbed. "Real clean. 'Til last weekend when I went to a party and some guy I didn't even know offered me a drag on his weed."

"Well, that isn't so bad, Georgia." I moved closer to her.

"Not so bad until your bottom feeder here took pictures of me smoking the dope. I begged him not to give them to anybody, to sell them to me. His price was way too high even for my morals."

At that moment, I hated Cal for what he did. I'd always trusted him.

The gun lay in her lap almost forgotten. I took my opportunity and lunged forward, reaching for the weapon, but the little girl was too quick for my middle-aged knees. I watched her grab the Glock and she turned it on me again. "See how you lie! You all lie and cheat for the almighty buck!"

The gun exploded. For an instant I figured I was dead, until a limp white hand landed across my lap still holding the gun.

I could already see the headlines: "Hush-Hush Tells All! Georgia Maine Dies in Murder/Suicide Mystery."

A big seller.

WINTER SOLSTICE

THE SCHOOL cafeteria seemed overly quiet. Nan sat across from her best friend and fellow teacher, Muriel. The last bell of the afternoon had rung.

"You can't fool me, Nan. I've known you too long. Something happened in Hatteras this summer."

Nan blushed scarlet. "You always seem to know when I'm in trouble."

"So, there is something bugging you?"

"Not too much, just an old story, I guess. I met a wonderful man and made a fool of myself!"

"Aw, c'mon, Nan. I've never known you to ever make a fool of yourself. Let's talk."

Nan told Muriel that a Hilary and David Brown had rented the cottage next to hers at the beach. Hilary was very frail and in a wheel chair most of the time. She had multiple sclerosis.

"I didn't pay much attention to them at first. I just waved when I walked Missy on the beach. David stopped us once to talk."

"I'm crazy about golden retrievers," he said. "They're such active and entertaining dogs."

"He wanted to know what I named her and asked me if he could take a walk with us some evening. I didn't see any harm in that. That very evening he was there falling into step beside us."

"Our walks together got to be a regular thing and we talked about my being a teacher. He told me that he was a journalist. You know just getting acquainted stuff. Then, one evening, we were walking in our bare feet. It was so beautiful with the tide coming in. I picked up some shells to bring back to the kids here. When I looked up at him, he was appraising me with his eyes. I got so nervous, I thought I'd cry. After all, I'm no beauty! Too tall, too blonde, too robust..."

"C'mon, Nan, quit putting yourself down."

"Well, I was thinking, too, about his little wife. I started prattling on like a schoolgirl, about how I loved to write poetry. I've never told anyone about my poetry, not even you! The last evening I was there we were walking and I had let the dog off her leash to play in the water. Unexpectedly, he motioned to me to sit down beside him in the sand. He patted a place beside a patch of sea grass, putting his jacket down for me to sit on. He kissed me, easy and completely, as if we'd known each other forever. Oh, Muriel, I tried to resist, really. I told him, 'David, I can't do this. You're married and have responsibilities. I'm happy with my life, my singleness,' I lied."

"Nan, don't be so hard on yourself. Sometimes these things happen and we don't plan them. Don't blame yourself!" Muriel patted my hand as I tried to control my tears.

"He told me that I had come to mean more to him than he had ever thought possible. I wanted to run. It was hell and heaven both at the same time. It was the most wonderful night of my life! Now he's probably laughing about the *old maid school teacher* who was so easy!"

Christmas was a joy for Nan and the children made it very special for her with their gleeful energy. On the last day before Christmas vacation, a large white florist box was delivered to her in her classroom. Inside was one perfect red rose surrounded by sea grass. There was no card.

UNFORGIVEN

THE OLD LADY sat in a rocking chair by the window, moving her lips soundlessly. The morning sun straying over her limp white hair and dappling her parchment cheeks felt warm. Every few minutes she'd push with her feet. The rocking chair would creak its complaints at being disturbed. Like her it was old and colorless.

Gabrielle was eighty-one. She hadn't always been colorless. On her good days, the nurses would tell you, she was able to recall a time when she was frivolous and beautiful. Those days had lasted too briefly for her.

The blonde nurse would come into her room and pat her shoulder. "C'mon, Gabrielle, sing us a song this lovely morning." The old lady laughed a little at that. On her good days she could laugh a little. She liked the blonde nurse; she reminded Gabrielle of her long dead mother. "You're a caution," she'd whisper to the nurse.

On her bad days, Gabrielle Kent Cort lived the nightmare of her girlhood tragedy, remembering that hot August day that sin tainted her young life.

"Gabrielle! Don't go too far. Push your dolly buggy over by the barn and stay in sight. I have an errand for you to run."

The small girl, not quite nine, continued to push the baby buggy down the farm lane toward the barn.

"See, darling baby, how nice it is here under the poplars. When we get home, I'll feed you and put you in your cradle for a nap." The child pretended to cover the doll.

Her mother's voice intruded. She pushed the buggy, raising dust to the back porch of the farmhouse.

Her mother, Lena Kent, came out. Her sweet, plump face, pink from the heat, as she carried a cloth sugar bag, lumpy with something inside.

"Carry this down to the creek and take care of it," she commanded the girl.

Gabrielle stood there; her big, blue eyes, the color of corn flowers, were wide with shock and disbelief. "Oh, no. No, Ma!" She backed away from her mother's reach.

"You listen to me, girl. There's nothing to it. Just hold the sack under the water until there's no more movement or bubbles."

"I can't do it, Ma." Tears streaked down her face. "Don't the Bible say it's a sin to kill, Ma?"

"This isn't the same as what the Bible meant; these are just another batch of the old tiger's kittens and I can't have any more cats around the barn. We're falling over them now. Just listen and do as you're told."

Gabrielle started to sob, throwing herself down on the porch steps. "It's a sin, Ma! You know it's a sin!"

Lena, not used to having any of her eight children cross her, soberly and with much strength, pulled the child to her feet. She opened the small-fisted hand and wrapped the hand around the top of the sugar bag. "Now, no more foolishness, get going!"

Defeated, the little girl walked toward the creek.

There had been other times when older brother, Joe, had been dispatched to the creek with a bag to drench. It hadn't seemed so shocking then, when someone else did the deed. No one seemed to think much about it. Why didn't they think about it? Why didn't people care when little, helpless kittens were drowned? Gabrielle felt confused and frightened.

When the girl celebrated her eighteenth birthday, Lena was so proud of her daughter. On the same day, she announced Gabrielle's engagement to Densel Cort, a young lawyer from nearby Oceola.

Lena's pride shone.

The young lovers had met in church where Gabrielle Kent spent much of her time as a choir member and Sunday school teacher.

Everyone commented to Lena about the girl's wonderful and constant commitment to her faith and her church. "She's always been very religious," Lena would repeat. "We started to notice her religious bent when she was about nine or ten."

The marriage produced three strong girls. Even though Densel would tell her how happy he was after each daughter was born, she knew he desperately wanted a son.

Their fourth child was born on a cold February day. It was a boy. He lived five hours.

Everyone grieved, but Gabrielle was silent and pale. No tears, no emotion shown. Only silence. When the tiny coffin was lowered into the ground, Gabrielle, wooden and colorless, walked away from the group as condolences were still being given to Densel. When the family noticed she was missing, they searched until dusk.

Densel found her floating face down and nearly dead in the cold creek.

"Gabby!" He worked over her, rubbing her hands, patting her face. "Speak to me, darling. Please, speak to me," he begged.

A low moan escaped her lips.

"I have sinned! I have sinned! I have sinned!" Over, and over, and over she said it.

Gabrielle Kent Cort died in the Cannonport Sanitarium on a warm August day in 1985. She had resided there since her fiftieth birthday, suffering major depression.

Her girls stood by her bed. Her lips moved... "Mama, it is a sin."

A SOFT PLACE TO FALL

WYNONNA'S lusty, sultry voice emanates from my disc player as she sings her latest new song, "What the World Needs Now is Love." It demands my attention making me sway, and, oddly enough, I think of Penny—not her real given name of Penelope, which she hates.

Penny is my daughter, that is when she acts like it, which isn't often. She's sixteen years old and thinks she owns the world.

Wynonna continues to croon about love. I hear only a few words.

Penny's face is in front of my eyes. I see her bluer than blue eyes, large, defiant now, her face white with powder, black lipstick on her lips. Lips that seem to have forgotten how to smile.

She mocks me with her clothes. Knowing how I always bought her sunny, bright colors to wear, she wears nothing but black. God knows where she gets the stuff. It's hopeless to ask anymore.

The music continues to drift on: "I will be free." The phrase from the song makes me tear up. Isn't that what Penny had screamed at me for so long? "Leave me alone. I want to be free. I want to do my own thing."

A telephone call to her father across town gives me nothing to hang on to. He might as well be on the other side of the continent for all he cares about her anymore. Anymore? Never! He never did care about us.

Why I continue to play the charade of calling out to him for help is beyond me. I should know better.

"Kick her ass out!" he says. That's supposed to solve it.

He doesn't know that sometimes Penny stands outside his new home at night just to get a peek at him.

I discovered that one night, when I followed the car after her friends picked her up. The kid driving left her out on the corner near her father's house and drove away. She stood in the shadow of a big pine tree near the house just watching. I sat in my car, a distance away, crying bitter tears for a while. Then I drove away so she wouldn't see me. I prayed that she'd come home that night. She didn't.

Trying to understand my child when she says, "I just want to be me," baffles me. She hasn't the vaguest idea of who that *me* is.

"Can't we talk about things?" I asked her.

"What things?" she spits back.

"We could talk about what we can do to make us happy with each other again."

"What good would it do? You never listen to me."

I remember getting angry at that. "Never listen to you? You never listen to me. I've told you over and over again that you're heading for trouble."

"Okay, then it's my trouble."

"No, that's one of the things you refuse to understand. Your trouble is my trouble. I love you Penny, and it's me who has to come to your rescue when you mess things up for yourself."

"There you go blaming me for *things* again. Can't you just forget it?"

"Talk to me. Please."

"I ain't got anything to say."

"Oh, baby, please talk to me... be my little girl again." I can't help it, I cry out loud.

She smashed the large photograph of herself that was taken when she was twelve. My favorite picture of her. She threw it to the floor then ground her booted heel into it before she ran out the front door.

That was six weeks ago. When I'm home from work, I try to keep busy doing little things to keep my mind off of my missing child.

I did everything I could think of to find her. First calling her father, just in case, knowing that would be fruitless. Then, I called around to all of her few friends, the ones you feel are weird... the ones who hold her secrets because they're just like her.

Then I called the police. They treat you like you're slightly foolish. "She'll come back Mrs. James," they said. "They usually come back after a few weeks, when they need a soft place to fall."

Eight weeks went by. The doorbell alarmed me out of my thoughts about my daughter. Two policemen stood at my door showing me their badges.

"Mrs. James, we might have found Penny. Could you come down to the station and talk to us?"

"What do you mean you might have found her? Did you find her?"

"We're not sure. Please put on a coat and ride down to the station with us."

While I was getting my coat, the disc player was playing Wynonna's "Your Day Will Come."

I crossed the room and turned it off. I wondered to myself what day had come for me.

Standing beside the steel drawer in the morgue, I gazed at my child's face in death. Somehow, in my misery, I couldn't help thinking that here, in this place, there was not a soft place to fall.

IF YOU CAN'T STAND THE HEAT

I WATCHED Joe sweat his life away in the kitchen of Joey's Barbecue. Sometimes I felt like a Hindu widow who'd been sentenced to practice suttee every living day of my life, sacrificing my youth and middle-age to the premise that the business must come first. The constantly hot pyres that were the barbecue racks sputtered and spit heat at me most of my days.

Joe, or Joey, as his acquaintances called him, was totally committed to his stores. Nothing else was to interfere, not even me, his wife of twenty years.

I tried. "Let's go away, Joe. Let's have a little fun for a few days."

He just looked at me like I was crazy.

Joe was a true black man. He walked the walk and talked the talk. I was a white woman in a black man's world, but that part never bothered me. I'd been raised in a mixed neighborhood, and if you can't learn your lessons that way, you never will.

I fought my fights and met Joe in junior high school. His gentleness and high hopes for a future had turned me into a believer. "We're gonna make it, Franny. All we got to do is keep our noses to the ground and save our money."

It had all come true for him. The hard work, the saving, sacrificing, and the deprivations that our marriage endured had all paid off for him.

Not for me.

I learned to keep the books, and each month, as the business grew, Joe looked less and less at me, and more and more at the figures in those books.

If You Can't Stand the Heat

Looking back on it all now, maybe I didn't know how good I had it.

Maybe I should remember more of the good times when we used to sit together after the first store opened.

Joe'd lock up for the night and we'd sit in an empty booth and plan our futures. We'd dream of a new house, a new, clean life away from the neighborhood, the guns and cockroaches.

"I want kids...three or four kids!" Joe's eyes seemed to glaze over at the mere mention. "Maybe later." The same answer came year after year, until I was obsessed with the idea of having kids.

When Bill Ward entered our lives, it didn't seem to make any noticeable impact on us. To Joe he was just another hand to train on the stairway to Joe's success. To me, he was just a white man in our black world.

"How do, Miz Tyler." His blue eyes always seemed to sparkle. He was quiet and polite to me. "Mighty pretty dress you have on."

I don't know how it started, exactly. He just started talking to me in his quiet way while he cooked or cleaned up.

I would sit at my kitchen desk in the store, trying to concentrate on the numbers.

At first, it was about the store. Then, the talk slowly changed to where he'd been and what he'd done. "You might say I've had a checkered career!" he said, as he shook the red and white checkered tablecloth from the nearest table.

We'd laugh together. It got easier for me to laugh with Bill around. I got to thinking it'd been a long time since Joe and I had laughed together.

Then one day, Joe said he had to go to San Francisco to look at some new equipment. He left Bill to run the store and me to look over his shoulder making sure all went according to Hoyle.

When we closed that night, Bill and me, there was no thought of any wrongdoing in our heads. Bill just looked at me with those laughing eyes and said, "Listen, Franny, it's been a long day. Let's stop somewhere for a cold drink."

"O.K.," I answered. My knees were a bit wobbly just thinking of going with Bill. But hell, I thought, why not?

I was scared after that first evening. Afraid Joe'd find out. Afraid I'd go again. Afraid of myself mostly.

"Franny, why not go to market with me on Monday?" Bill's soft voice encouraged me.

"No, I'd better hang around here. Joe's going to be in Frisco again."

"C'mon, you deserve a break, and anyhow, we're closed."

It started a routine. Joe gone on business on Mondays. Me meeting Bill's truck at the mall entrance to be with him all day. I hated myself!

After six months of deceit, I tried to end it. "Don't ask me anymore, Bill. Just forget it. If Joe finds out, we're dead."

But, the next Monday morning I stood outside the mall entrance waiting for the green pick-up truck. I couldn't quit and neither could Bill.

Joe could have melted into the grease of the French-fryer for all I ever saw of him, until one night he rolled his head toward me in bed and asked me right out, "Who you seein'?"

My throat went dry. I couldn't speak.

"I may be a dumb nigger about some things, but not so dumb I can't tell my wife's steppin'."

Finding my voice, "If I was, would you even care?" I breathed it. "You haven't cared for a long time. How long do you think I'd be satisfied to screw around with just your books?"

Joe jumped out of bed like he'd been electrocuted and bounded toward the dresser. I knew I'd gone too far. The lights flashed on and I was looking into the eyes of a madman, all red and bloodshot.

"Oh God! Oh God! Oh God," I screamed, jumping for the door.

Then I was stopped cold by Joe's voice, all cool and oily. "I'm gonna kill you, woman." This was a Joe I'd never seen before. "But before I do, you're going to tell me who it is."

The gun was black and heavy. Even in his hands, it trembled.

I thought of Bill and the fate that was in store for him if I told. In those minutes I had to be honest with myself... it wasn't all Bill's fault. I coulda' said no.

He stepped close and hit me across the face with the gun. I couldn't feel anything. It was the first time he'd ever struck me. I fell to my knees sobbing, "It isn't anyone you know... No one you know..."

Blood was running down my forehead blinding me. "I loved you Joe, but you forgot about me... be honest with yourself. You don't love me anymore. That was lost a long time ago."

"You were my woman, Franny... my woman."

"Like the stores you own?"

"It was for you." You could tell by his voice he knew it was a lie. He put the gun carefully into the dresser drawer.

I ran into the bathroom and grabbed a towel to try and stop the flow of blood. As I looked at myself in the mirror, I heard the front door close softly.

It was ended.

> *"Here's another fine mess you've gotten me into."* –Oliver Hardy (1892-1952)

SISTERS

A SMALL eight-year-old girl named Spryte is busy turning cartwheels across the manicured grass between the gravestones. Her long blonde curls bob and wave like a large mop's head. Each time she hits the ground with a thump, she yells back over her shoulder toward her older sister, "See, I'm better at this than you are!" It seemed to be very important to Spryte that she be better than her older sister, Faith, at all things. She stuck her tongue out at her sister for further emphasis.

Faith, trying very hard to ignore the veiled challenge to participate, continues to help her mother arrange peonies on their grandmother's grave. A sober, reflective child of 10, Faith really wants to join her sister and try her hand at cartwheels. She knew Mama wouldn't like it.

Estelle awakens to a lily-of-the-valley kind of day in April.

Sitting up, she listens to the tumult above her.

"Someone's dancing on my grave!" she wails.

She rubs her eyes then runs her fingers through her long, unruly brown hair. "Gawd!" she mutters, "will this stuff ever stop growing?" Then, giggling to herself, she thinks about her old hairdresser, Ramone. Ramone sitting in his fancy salon, gooing up the heads of the local junior leaguers to shine, kink, flip and bleach into imitations of some celebrity they fancied. Ramone, wisely agreeing each new "do" is, indeed, THEM!

Wouldn't he just die if I walked in for a haircut? Her amusement fades as the thumps overhead increase in intensity.

"Sherry! Sherry! Wake up! Don't you hear all that noise? I tell you, someone is dancing on my grave! Sherry!"

Through the muddy wall, a sweet voice answers, "Oh, Estelle, settle down. Can't I ever have any peace when you're around?"

"You listen to me, dear Sherry; you're the one who put us here."

"How can you say that, Estelle?"

"I can say that because it's true. You always took whatever you wanted of mine. You even tried to steal David from me on the eve of our betrothal. You were always the favorite."

"I never tried to steal anyone from you. Could I help it if David told me he wanted me and not you?"

"In your dreams, bitch!"

"Just for the record, Estelle, it was you who jerked the steering wheel over and sent us off the cliff. It was your unreasonable jealousy that caused that fight. Always jealousy. Jealousy of me, and Mama, jealousy that lost you David, too. I'm going back to sleep, sister dear, and so should you."

"Damn you, Sherry, and your selfish attitude. If I'm going to be tortured here with that noise up there, you're not going to sleep through it. You're going to share it."

"Why must you always be so irritable, even here?" Sherry begins to think of a lovely white cloud, picturing herself walking toward the azure blue of the distant sky. She hears Estelle pounding on the wall again.

"I'm going up there and put a stop to this stuff."

"Don't be absurd. You can't go up there."

"Oh, no? We'll see about that."

Spryte's mother calls out to her to stop the acrobatics.

"Faith, go over there, darling, and tell your sister I want her to show more respect while we're here in the cemetery."

Faith walks toward her sister, a self-satisfied smirk on her face, "Mama says for you to stop being such a dummy and quit acting like a baby, jumping around." Not waiting for an argument, Faith returns to her mother's side.

Spryte, tiring of her sport, lies down, resting her head on the marble pillow stone that marks the graves of the sisters, Estelle and Sherry.

Cut into the marble: MAY MY BELOVED DAUGHTERS REST IN PEACE FOREVER.

Estelle forces her stiff, bony legs to stand. Then, adjusting her white shroud, she inhales and reaches for the unseen sky. She huffs and puffs with all her strength.

Winded and disheveled, she finds herself staring into the face of Spryte, lying there catching her breath.

"You will stop that noise. Do you have any idea how that sounds down there?" She points a bony finger hellward.

"Are you an angel?" Spryte gasps.

"Well, hardly."

"Then what are you?"

"Uh...uh...I am a fairy princess who likes her rights respected!"

Estelle smoothed her rumpled hair back and tried to act regal, holding her head up in a peculiar, austere fashion.

Spryte laughs and shows her dimples. "Gee whiz! That sounds pretty important."

Estelle feels unsure of herself for the first time in her life...or death.

Faith stands about a hundred feet away waving her hand and yelling, "C'mon. Mom says we're leaving 'cause you're such a dope!"

Spryte's attention turns to Faith and fails to observe Estelle turn to vapor.

Turning back to the spot where Estelle had stood, she searches the ground closely with her eyes. Nothing there.

Then running toward her sister she calls out, "Did you see her? Did you see the…uh…fairy princess?"

Faith observes Spryte's impish eyes. "No, I didn't see any fairy princess and neither did you, so quit trying to put one over on me. Let's go."

Spryte opens her mouth to answer, thinks better of it, and just pouts.

Estelle is almost sorry she forced herself to come out and be seen. Shouldn't have done that. She shivers in the cool spring breeze, the shroud is thin. Hugging herself, she inhales deeply wishing to rejoin Sherry below. Closing her eyes, Estelle exhales deeply again and makes a dive for beneath. The ground is hard and unyielding. She hits her nose. "Ouch!" Rubbing her nose furiously, she feels desperation for the first time.

Estelle even feels desperate to see Sherry.

Perhaps, she thinks, if I balance myself on the pillow stone for a higher dive I can crack through.

While Estelle thinks, she fails to see Spryte tiptoe up toward her with cautious steps.

"Are you here, Princess? I can't see you."

Estelle jumps over the granite stone and falls to the ground. "Damn…Damn…Damn!" she screeches.

"I hear you, I hear you." Spryte is getting excited.

Estelle hides behind the child.

"Won't you let me show you to my sister?" Just then a cool gust of wind rattles the new foliage on the trees nearby, and as Spryte turns to look, she catches a glimpse of Estelle whirling like a dervish into a smoky mist.

The little girl stands very still looking for the image and listening hard.

"GO HOME!" a voice commands near her ear.

Spryte skips back to her impatient mother, while Estelle breathes a sigh of relief.

As the car bearing the three visitors passes, the child, hanging out of the rear window, whispers, "I'll be back." Estelle hears it on the wind and shudders.

Getting back to the business of returning to where she belongs, she pulls her shroud tightly around her, blows out all of the air in her lungs, then inhales until she feels like a balloon about to take flight. Leaping straight up into the air, she turns over in a perfect half gainer, toes pointed, then disappears into space.

Arriving shaken and repentant, back in her resting place, she calls softly, "Sherry, dear."

"What, for heaven's sake!"

Estelle is relieved to hear her sister's soft voice again. "I was up there for a few minutes."

Sherry, always the lady of the two, answers sweetly from the other side of the muddy wall, "In your dreams, bitch!"

FOR LOVE

JUDITH DIMSLEY sat in the front row of the small courtroom. Her face was a study in grief and disbelief. The jury of eight men and four women had just returned their verdict. The foreman, a small, bony man of about sixty, stood straight and held a paper firmly, "We, the jury, find Jake Turner guilty of murder in the first degree."

Judith closed her eyes, afraid to meet Jake's woeful gaze. *It couldn't be*, she thought. *He never killed Jason and Myra Coolidge. He never entered their home with a gun, in broad daylight, and shot them both to death.*

She knew that as well as she knew her own name.

Sheriff Millard Beardsley had hauled Jake Turner into his office to question him. They said he was the last person seen, or almost seen, at the Coolidge house. He failed to convince them that the truck seen in front of the house where the murders were committed was not his white truck. Jake swore he hadn't been near the place, that he had been with a lady most of the afternoon when the killing occurred. He would not name the lady.

Turner's truck, a sad, beat-up white Nissan of some years, was impounded. Still, a neighbor of the Coolidge family, Loretta Phillips, insisted, as she pushed heavily tinted glasses up on her long nose, that the truck was Turner's.

The sheriff questioned Loretta about what she saw. "How can you be so sure that the truck you saw belonged to Jake Turner?"

"I've seen that truck travelin' all around town for years. Everyone knows Jake Turner never held a day job like most of the decent men in this town." Even though her eyesight was questionable, the sheriff chose to accept her identification of the white truck. Added to that, a bit of information was under an old paint tarp in the back of Turner's truck. They found a work shirt with what looked like blood splatters on it. They sent the shirt into the state capital labs for testing.

If the blood belonged to either of the Coolidges, they had their man.

Three days after the forensic testing of the bloody shirt, word was faxed to the sheriff. It was human blood. That was all they could determine because it had been rain-soaked in a rusty pool of water too long to get DNA.

When Jake was questioned about the shirt, he told them he had butchered a deer in that shirt.

The county prosecutor was disappointed with the evidence, but felt that he could still get a conviction with the eyewitness testimony of the half-blind Phillips woman. He had done just that.

Judith Dimsley was a woman in her early fifties. An elementary school teacher. Considered by most of the townspeople as the typical spinster with a cat. She was almost invisible to the Centerville folks. Her dull life had taken a quick turn when Jake Turner started calling on her. He was thirty-five and had never lost his heart, never had a real girlfriend until he met Judith. He was completely taken with her gentleness, the careful way she spoke to him, her quiet hazel eyes, and her honesty.

Judith saw Jake as a strong protector, a man that appreciates the good earth and preserving it, someone she could trust with her life and her love. A ruggedly handsome Apollo.

They met when Jake came around to fix the door hinges on her storm door. Besides being a handyman, Jake was also adept at hunting deer and pheasant, often taking less knowledgeable, novice hunters into the woods to show them how it's done.

The fact that Turner did not hold a steady job was used against him at trial. The gossips would have been even more tsk-tisking during their idle gossip if they knew he was really in love with the spinster, Judith Dimsley. He wasn't going to give them more fodder for their cannons.

The day after he was indicted, Judith went to the Sheriff to tell him that Jake had been at her house fixing a roof leak. He'd been there all afternoon. He didn't have the time to do the killing of the Coolidges. But, then there was the bloody shirt to explain away! They ignored her story completely.

The world stopped spinning for the school teacher when the verdict was read. "*Guilty*" echoed in her ears. What could she do to change that, she asked herself.

Two weeks later the sentencing hearing was opened. The Judge, Amos J. Bender, looked at Jake standing before him. He adjusted his glasses as he started to berate Jake about the cold-blooded crime he was found guilty of committing. He pronounced the death sentence for Jake Turner.

Judith fainted dead away and had to be carried from the courthouse by the emergency squad. After reviving her, they said they would take her to the local hospital if she liked.

She didn't like, and was delivered home.

The day before Jake was to be transferred to the state penitentiary and death row, Judith was allowed to visit with him, bars between them, at the county jail. Their conversation was whispered, unheard by the guard, who couldn't have cared less anyway. The brief visit ended with Jake reaching through the bars squeezing the spinster's hand. Then she put her face close to his and kissed his lips.

Two muffled shots were heard by the guard. He hurried toward Judith who was wilting onto the floor, a gun in her small hand. Two minutes later Jake and Judith were both dead.

Centerville was never the same after that. There were questions to be answered. How did she get the gun past the guard? Did he search her when she arrived? He swore he had. How did she get the gun into the jail? They're still pondering that one.

An explosion of news people brought a media frenzy. The town's people were perplexed about the relationship between Judith and Jake. First, it was a scandal. Then it became a tragedy and, with time, it has become a strange but sad love story.

Judith Dimsley would have liked that.

THE RIALTO

AFTER TWENTY YEARS of lying in dust and cobwebbed shadows, the old Rialto Theater was going to reopen its doors to the public again. Like visions of sugarplums dancing through my mind or promises of an early spring, it sounded wonderful to me.

Talk about playing the Palace! During my prepubescent years, I think I must have seen every Friday night mystery movie, Saturday cowboy matinee and Sunday, Technicolor musical that played the Rialto. That's saying a lot... that's seeing a lot!

Movies didn't book into the neighborhood theaters for weeks back then. The country's hunger for the depression-beaters saw the marquees changed about three times a week by some teenager stepping to dizzying ladder-heights, teetering there, slipping letters into their proper places. Friday, Saturday and Sunday, the letters were changed every day. Sometimes the letter changer ran out of the needed letters leaving the marquee signs looking like toothless combs. DRUMS ALONG TH MOHAK, or BRODWAY MEODY of 1937! Never mind, we knew the titles from the coming attractions that titillated our imaginations and drew us back for more excitement.

From the closet-sized confectionery next door to the theater, there wafted aromatic clouds of buttered popcorn scent. Like automatons, we kids followed our feet into the store to spend our dimes on popcorn and our nickels on Milk Duds. Then, laden with our goodies, we'd head for the ticket booth to offer our

The Rialto

fifteen cents to a sweet-faced cashier who punched the ticket machine so that it burped out our tickets up and across the counter in a measured hiccup.

I got my first kiss in the Rialto. I was ten and my partner in crime was eleven and smelled like licorice. The son of the chief of police in our suburban town, I remember him riding up to my house on his bike on Friday afternoons to inform me that he was going to the movie for the Saturday matinee.

"Are you going?" he asked, in an offhand manner.

"Uh huh." I nodded my head.

"See you there, then." And away he rode.

He grew up friendly and handsome and lost both legs in Europe during the Second World War.

By the time I was in the sixth grade, the more popular boys in the class started to meet on Friday evenings in front of the old theater. The popular girls soon joined in the meeting and the two groups would line up for tickets, then enter the dark auditorium en masse, occupying the back left-hand side of the rear block of seats. There they sat through the movie, eating, making wisecracks, and cracking gum while the girls giggled a lot.

The usher, his flashlight flying over the group like an errant firefly, would shush them, "Quiet, quiet.... Keep it down or out you go!" I never did see anyone put out.

Under the darkened and dusty draped dome of the Rialto, I cut my teeth on *Dracula,* often thanking my lucky stars that he wasn't cutting his teeth on me!

In the make-believe place that was the movie house, I felt my heart sing with Bing Crosby in the *Bells of St. Mary's*, my dreams flourish in fantasy dances with Fred Astaire and Ginger Rogers, and my dreams form as I watched my idol, Eleanor Powell.

She tap-danced her way through arches, down stairs and over drums. How I wished to be like her.

I lost my heart over and over again to *Zorro*, *Flash Gordon*, *Tarzan* and finally to my great teen-love Van Johnson, whose wavy strawberry-blond hair, freckled face and agile body made him so handsome in military uniforms as he walked across the bubblegum speckled silver screen of the Rialto straight into my young heart.

I can still feel the lumps of dried chewing gum that ossified under the arms of the seats. Later theater owners refused to sell chewing gum in their refreshment stands.

Along with the fun of the old theater, there was sometimes real pathos.

Sammy, a teenager noted for playing football on the high school team, was an avid movie-goer preferring to attend and sit in the very last row of the Rialto on Saturday afternoons for the Westerns. I'm sure he'll never forget his experience in the place.

He was sitting in his favorite seat one Saturday matinee next to another ardent fan, an old lady who loved the Western movies and was well known by sight to all the kids. Halfway through the first movie of a double feature, Sammy heard a slight thud near his feet on the floor. Reaching down he retrieved the woman's purse and just laid it on her lap, continuing to view the movie uninterrupted. Moments later the thud sounded again and the young man once more retrieved the purse placing it on her lap. The third time alerted him to the fact that something must be wrong. He discovered that his venerable seat partner was quite dead! She had expired somewhere in the middle of a Tom Mix shoot-out. What a way to go!

It's no wonder that the night the Rialto reopened, I stepped into the place feeling a "rush" I'd forgotten I could feel. I even shed a few tears, quickly blinked back so the crowd around wouldn't see them. The old movie house was still filled with ghosts and memories for me and wonderful promises of coming attractions.

A SWALLOW'S PLACE

I WANT TO WALK into the picture. Feel the snow with my fingers, rub it on my warm face.

I want to journey back to that place in time. To feel the icy wind paint my cheeks and nose red. Flail the axe again, the one sticking into the old tree stump, until my shoulders ache. I want to hide once more in the old barn where swallows swoop so elegantly after their insect quarry and trill their successes. I gaze at the album in my lap...the picture of the place I'll always call home. I hear old echoes.

"Jenny! Jenny! You answer me, girl!"

The straw tickles my nose. Old Bess makes finicky noises beside me, her hooves nervous.

I whisper to her from beneath the straw. "Now, now, Bess, it's all right."

I poke one hand out of the pile of straw and stroke her leg softly. She gentles down a bit.

Listening for Mother's call again, I feel the wind seep through the barn siding. Her voice is carried once more to me on the wind.

"Jenny Lou Carter, you get yourself in here and quit trying to hide. I know you're in the barn. Don't make me come after you."

Never, ever, going to let her catch me. Never, never, never going to leave here.

The tears seem to come without permission; I stick my tongue out and catch a salty stream running down my face. Shimmying up old Bess's hind end, I use her tail like a rope. The mule never moves.

My overalls are stiff with mud and cold. My red hair hangs in strings down my back, straight and

A Swallow's Place

damp. The old mule swings her soft muzzle sideways toward me as I sit astride her bare back. She's looking all kinds of questions my way.

"Okay, girl, let's go!" I lean over and open the stall gate.

She walks forward, my hands buried in her mane guiding her toward the barren, snow-covered lane.

Except for the wind gusting now and then, there is deep soft silence. Then Bess' hooves beat a muffled tattoo over the snow as we both breathe a trail of foggy vapors behind us.

We circle the small farm, the mule and me, not sure where to go. How do you leave a place you don't want to leave, ever?

A predicament for me. At ten years of age, I feel very grown up and at the same time very young.

Ever since Pa died, I knew this day would come. Ma kept telling me, "We will have to give up the farm, Jenny. I can't keep it going alone."

"I'll help. I'll do everything you say, Ma."

It was no use. The resignation was in her eyes.

Bad enough that Pa left us, now Ma wants to give up our place. I knew I'd fight to stay. How could I ever leave old Bess?

"We're in this together, old friend. You don't want me to leave here and move in with Aunt Hettie, do you?"

The mule tosses her head a little, enjoying the freedom.

"I knew you didn't."

We didn't see it coming. Bess drops out from under me, I topple to the hard ground, my left side racked by pain. I scream.

The old spring hole cover protrudes from the ground rotted and useless. The hole open deep and black. Poor Bess is half in the deep hole and half out. The animal's whinnying is filled with fright and pain.

How long have we been downed? I'm so cold. Bess is still.

I hear the rusty Chevy station wagon as it grunts and groans over the field laboring its way to us. What took them so long? It's almost dark.

Ma and Uncle Jake are fussing over me. Ma is touching my legs, my arms.

"Ouch! Don't touch my arm," I protest. I can hear Ma whisper to Jake, "It's broken!"

Ma cradles my head against her chest. She smells like Lily of the Valley perfume. She tells me to be still until Uncle Jake can lift me into the car.

Jake goes over to Bess, then scuffs the frozen dirt furrow a second.

Returning to Ma and me he reports, "The mule won't make it." He says it in a matter-of-fact way.

"It's my fault, my fault..." I strike the frozen ground with my good fist.

"Now, now, Jenny, try not to think about it." Jake lifts me into the station wagon.

He walks back to Bess and puts her down with his deer rifle.

I want to die.

Ma tells me to try and forget about it. I'll never forget.

In my own room, in my own bed, there's no feeling of victory that I managed to postpone our move to Hettie's for a few weeks. I feel defeated and guilty.

Looking out of the window, I can see the barn paintless and grey. An old rundown barn full of memories of Bess and me and childhood.

Now, here, thirty years later, I hold the album looking at the old photograph Pa took. The one from the lane at the farm after a record snow. Still, I wish I could walk into that time again for just a little while and tell Bess I'll never forget her. Not ever.

You might also enjoy Alice Louise's breakout novel:

***THE PINK RIBBON** – A Tale of Romance, Tragedy, and Triumph*

THE PINK RIBBON is set in the verdant Allegheny Mountains in the 1850s.

The life of Matthew Gallio reached from the coal mines of those storied mountains to the streets of Paris, France. Born into poverty, of immigrant parents, he was orphaned at age ten. Gifted as an artist, he rose to unbelievable fame as a portrait painter. Tragedy, deceit, and love are woven into his quest for happiness.

Three women loved him, and each in her own way shaped the saga of The Pink Ribbon: a coal miner's daughter, the daughter of a mine owner, and the beautiful granddaughter of his rich benefactress. His love for one of them would change his life forever.

Hatred, greed, and jealousy will plague Matthew throughout his career. His search for the love of his life is rewarded with disappointment and sorrow. Will his fame sustain him?

The Pink Ribbon is available in the Kindle Bookstore at Amazon.com and through other fine retailers.

> "A beautiful engaging read from first page to the last..."
> *–luvmykindle*

> "Felt the joy and pain of the characters."– *Marleen L.*

> "I could not put it down." *–Sally*

Soon to be published: Alice Louise's first anthology of poetry, ***A Universe of Verses***.

Made in the USA
Monee, IL
18 January 2020